I0656284

Secondary Readers 8

Beauty Queen

Secondary Readers

Beauty Queen

Barbara Kimenye

EAST AFRICAN EDUCATIONAL PUBLISHERS
Nairobi • Kampala

Published by
East African Educational Publishers Ltd.
Brick Court, Mpaka Road/Woodvale Grove
Westlands
P.O. Box 45314
Nairobi

East African Educational Publishers Ltd.
Pioneer House, Jinja Road
P.O. Box 11542
Kampala

© Barbara Kimenye 1997
First published 1997

ISBN 9966-46-014-4

Electronic typesetting by Jarodi Educational Institute
P.O. Box 38986 Nairobi.

Printed in Kenya by English Press Ltd.
Enterprise Road, P.O Box 30127 Nairobi.

Introduction

I am indebted to Dr. Sati Ghataura of Nairobi, Kenya, for giving so much of her valuable time to describing both the common and variable symptoms of Aids, the ways in which the disease can progress, and how, simply because of the physical structure of the female genitalia, women are far more at risk of contracting the virus from a single sexual encounter with an HIV-carrier than are men.

The message of this book, which has also been read and checked for medical facts by Dr. Ghataura, is therefore addressed specifically to girls who have reached the age of finding themselves very interested in, and of growing interest to members of the opposite sex.

On the whole it is a sad message intended to add to the general awareness that this rampaging killer disease is no respecter of persons and is capable of spreading like wildfire in ways other than through sexual intercourse.

There is no attempt in this book to provide advice or answers to the problems. 'Single Grazing' with no wandering into pastures new, is a commendable slogan in Uganda's campaign against Aids. But did you realise that in countries with ever-rising percentages of HIV-carriers, 'single grazing' offers no guarantee that one of the partners in a faithful relationship is not already and unknowingly HIV positive? There is nothing else for it: individuals must work out their own salvation.

Finally, Dr. Ghataura expressed herself as somewhat distressed by the final chapters of the book. Having witnessed Aids in all its harrowing stages, and seen the ostracizing and neglect to which some Aids victims have been subjected, she is a strong advocate of tender loving care on the part of relatives and friends. Dr. Ghataura points out that provided contact with the patient's bodily fluids is avoided, there is no risk of infection from a patient living normally as part of the family, even to the giving of comforting hugs and other gestures of affection. She stresses that to people without hope of recovery, human understanding is as important as any medicine in reducing their suffering.

Chapter 1

When the organiser triumphantly waved card number 7 above his head, and Adela with shock realised that it was also the number she wore attached to a ribbon on her wrist, she felt vaguely sick and went hot all over.

"Go on – you've won!" Her friend, Keti, excitedly gave her a push on to the rickety platform serving as a stage, while the other ten girls competing in the beauty contest varied their expressions from ill-concealed disappointment to false smiles of congratulations.

Minutes later Adela found herself standing awkwardly beside the organiser, to the noisy appreciation of an audience that grew noisier as a velvet cloak was draped around her shoulders, and a tinselled crown placed on her head to signify that she was now Miss Kabongo District.

"Walk around the stage to let the people have a good look at you," the organiser then hissed at Adela, frantically signalling at a group of musicians to play a suitable accompaniment.

It was a pity that musical accompaniment had not been given much thought in the run-up to the beauty contest. The group was insufficiently rehearsed as a unit, and their first attempt at a romantic melody was an ear-splitting discord until the lead guitarist got things under control.

Adela was too dazed and shy to be aware of the mess the musicians were making. She obediently walked a few paces then stood rooted to the spot, wishing the floor would open and swallow her up. She did not at all enjoy the wolf-whistles and crude personal remarks about her physical attractions that reached her from the mainly male audience. She wanted to run away and hide.

Luckily, her ordeal did not last long. The community hall at Kabongo Township was very basic in its amenities. While it boasted an apology of a stage, there were no curtains to close an event with a pretence of dignity, so anything taking place there usually ended up in a free-for-all. The beauty contest was no exception. As a panic-stricken

1

. members of the audience surged on-stage to mimic the girls who had aspired to be beauty queens...

Adela made a dash for where Keti and the other contestants were screened by a row of cupboards, the more agile members of the audience surged on-stage to mimic the girls who had aspired to be beauty queens, and fool around on the gilded throne.

Yoweri Wamala, the organiser, shook his head in despair. This chaotic finale was such a far cry from his ambitious dream of arranging his beauty competitions in a civilised and agreeable environment, with spotlit contestants parading to the strains of an accomplished orchestra, in front of an audience that knew how to behave.

As things stood, Yoweri was forced to make do with places practically identical to the Kabongo community hall, with their grimy walls plastered in Ministry of Health posters stressing the importance of vaccination against a variety of infant diseases, and warning against the deadly AIDS. The crowds attending these contests were invariably about as rough as their surroundings. It was little wonder, Yoweri sadly admitted, that he never attracted a better class of contestants than the local bar-girls and small-time prostitutes, or that he was sometimes reduced to pleading with respectable young women idling along the street to help swell the number of competitors.

Yoweri's biggest consolation was that he at least made an honest living from the contests he organised in semi-rural areas all over the country; not that they brought in anything like a fortune. Out of the small admission fee collected at the door came the cost of hiring the hall, the payment of a few local musicians, and prize money for the winner of the contest, which varied according to how much Yoweri had to spare after dealing with the other overheads.

Tonight's takings had been better than usual because Kabongo Township lay in the heart of a well-populated area lacking in regular entertainment. People had flocked from far and near to see the fun, and they hadn't seemed to mind sitting on the floor or perching on window ledges when the rows of folding chairs were fully occupied.

But with so many people swarming on-stage, Yoweri was unable to perform the usual closing ceremony of congratulating the winner and formally handing her the prize money (five hundred shillings, this time), and calling for a special round of applause for the losers for being such good sports. Instead, he hurriedly paid the musicians, then rushed to retrieve the crown, cloak and throne lest some thieving local got there before him. He then persuaded a couple of young boys to help load the throne onto the back of his pick-up, and he was about to drive off when he realised that a Mercedes Benz had partially blocked his path.

"Would you mind reversing a bit?" he shouted at somebody silhouetted against the bonnet of the car.

The gleaming end of a cigarette arched through the darkness as it was flung aside, then the person approached Yoweri and a head appeared at the open window on the driver's side of the pick-up. Yoweri switched on the cabin light and was surprised to see that the head belonged to a well-dressed, middle-aged man — not at all the type to normally patronise a semi-rural beauty contest.

"I didn't mean to be discourteous, sir," Yoweri said, humbled in the face of such obvious prosperity.

"That's all right, son," the man assured him. "You have probably had a very hard day. It can't be easy handling a show like this single-handed."

Yoweri eagerly nodded. "How right you are! I'm hoping that by next year . . . "

The man silenced him with a wave of his hand. "I'd really like to talk to you about this Miss Kabongo District. Adela, isn't it? That girl has great potential."

Yoweri frowned. "What do you mean by potential?" He was always very careful not to show the slightest familiarity in dealing with his contestants, regardless of many having questionable backgrounds, for he wanted no talk of his beauty queen business being a front for more sinister activities.

The man offered him his hand. "Joe Banda," he said by way of introduction. "I'm in the entertainment industry, and I think we could do something profitable with that girl." He glanced at the luminous dial of his watch. "Look. We can't talk here. How about meeting me at the Zebra bar in about fifteen minutes? I've got a proposition to put tc you."

Yoweri's face split in a broad grin. He sensed that here was his big chance. "I'll be there, sir!" he replied happily. "Call me Joe," Banda told him.

"Joe it is," Yoweri said, switching on the ignition and putting the pick-up in gear.

* * *

Meanwhile, Adela was on her way home with Keti, unaware that two men were about to take a hand in her future and ultimately decide her fate.

Leaving the community hall had proved a disturbing experience for the two girls. Local boys with whom they had played as children, who only a couple of days ago had pursued them from school with mocking cries of 'Spider legs!' and 'Mongoose nose!', had, outside the hall, displayed a startling change of attitude. The formerly mocking faces of those pressing in on them as Adela and Keti emerged from the hall had revealed a false desire to please, coupled with a clumsy gallantry that led to touching and groping. The effect on the girls was astonishment followed by outrage, and they had not hesitated to use their fists and feet in putting an end to such unexpected and completely unwanted interest before sprinting away up the road.

"I had great satisfaction in kicking Idwala's shins!" Keti breathlessly declared, as soon as they slowed to a walk. "That should teach him to keep his hands to himself in future!"

"Good for you," Adela panted. "And did you see the good thump I gave Wakumu when he tried to put his arm around my waist?"

"I can't understand why they should behave that way," Keti remarked. "That awful Duma, who has tormented us for as long as I can remember, had the nerve to grab my hand and call me 'sweetie'! Who does he think he is, I wonder?"

"You can bet your life that they had planned some special nastiness for us," Adela said. "All that pretending to be friendly. They probably think we got above ourselves when we entered the beauty competition."

Keti laughed. "It wasn't much of a competition, was it? I mean, that organiser pleading with us to enter so as to make up the numbers? I'm pretty sure that he had promised all the other girls that he would fix it for each one of them to win. You should have heard them talking when you went to be crowned! I suppose he didn't dare risk making any of those girls the winner after you got the most applause."

"I still can't understand how I came to win," Adela wondered aloud. "You are much prettier than I am, Keti, and some of the other girls were very smart. To be honest, I did not think that either of us stood any chance of winning, considering that 'we didn't have time to dress up. I mean look at this old cotton dress of mine! I've had it for ages!"

"Well, the audience must have thought you were special," Keti assured her. "What a pity that there was nobody from the newspapers to take your photograph."

"Oh, I'm glad there wasn't!" Adela exclaimed. "My parents would have a fit! As it is, I'll have a problem explaining how I came to enter the contest."

The girls parted at a crossroads to go their separate ways, and Adela walked along planning how to spend her unexpected windfall of five hundred shillings. She was slightly ashamed of not having offered to share it with Keti. After all, they shared most things, and Keti was definitely her best friend. Adela reached home, picturing Keti's delighted face were she, next morning, to hand her two hundred and fifty shillings; but the pleasant picture abruptly faded as she saw her father towering threateningly in the open doorway, and her mother anxiously hovering behind him.

"What have you been up to, you disgusting little slut?" he spat the words out, and Adela instinctively shrank away from him. Not even Keti was aware of how Adela's formerly mild parent had recently changed into a bullying monster, ready to lash out in response to what he considered lack of respect for his authority.

"I'm talking to you — answer me!" he roared, and as she started to tremble the flat of his hand caught her a stinging blow at the side of the head, sending her reeling.

"Oh, no . . . " her mother ineffectually protested.

Ignoring this weak interference, he again struck his daughter. "Beauty queen, is it?" he stormed. "I'll give you beauty queen, you whore! Fourteen-years-old and parading your body along with a crowd of common prostitutes! Josafat Kiringi couldn't get here fast enough to gloat over the sight of a daughter of mine shaming our whole family!"

He followed this up with a series of punches until Adela collapsed sobbing across the threshold, then with a final kick he strode angrily into the house.

Adela's mother, also sobbing by this time, helped her daughter to her feet and led her to her bedroom.

"I'm not staying here!" Adela rebelliously muttered through swollen lips, while her bruises and abrasions were attended to, and she was persuaded to drink a glass of hot milk.

"Now, now," her mother murmured, "your father only wants what's best for you. He's naturally upset because he feels that you have shamed us all. Whatever possessed you, child, to enter a beauty contest? Don't you know that only the lowest type of girl goes in for that sort of thing?"

Adela tried to explain. "We — Keti and I, that is — only did it as a joke. The organiser asked us to do it as a favour because he was short of contestants. Neither of us expected to win."

Her mother shook her head and looked mournful. "Joke or not, I thought that we had brought you up to value virtue and modesty. Girls whose vanity allows them to flaunt themselves in beauty contests are heading for disaster."

"But it wasn't at all like that!" Adela protested. "In any case, the organiser told us that the contest was to raise funds for charity. If you must know, mother, it was a bit like a school concert — only I'm sure the nuns would have organised it better!"

Her mother sighed. "That is not the point. Can't you see how bad it is to be judged solely on appearance? It encourages completely wrong values. Your father and I want you to grow up as a good Christian girl with self-respect and . . ."

"Oh, mother!" Adela had heard enough. She burrowed deep beneath the bedclothes and blocked her ears against any further recriminations.

In spite of the aches and pains received at the hands and feet of her father, she was tired out by the evening's excitement and quickly fell asleep. She was wandering in an unintelligible dream when a sweating, heavily-breathing body stole into her bed, and clumsy hands fumbled impatiently with the folds of *kanga* in which Adela was wrapped. Only as she sensed a rough urgency in the handling did she become wide awake, and then, as the horror of the situation dawned upon her, she let out a terrified scream.

Instantly, the big, clumsy body withdrew. Lights were switched on in other parts of the house, then Adela's mother and the maid Lucretia swiftly padded into her room, their faces reflecting a strangely furtive fear.

"She has had a nightmare," her mother hissed at Lucretia, noting the disordered sheets. "You go back to bed. I'll attend to her."

Lucretia hesitated for a moment, threw her mistress a glance of utter contempt, then turned and left the room. Adela feverishly clutched her mother's hand. "Father! It was father!" she whispered huskily. "I smelled his sweat, and he tried to . . ."

"Hush, child!" her mother quietly admonished. "You were dreaming. Your father is a good man. He would never harm you."

"It was father," Adela tearfully insisted but her mother shook her head.

"No. I promise you. Believe me, you were having a bad dream."

Adela said no more. She simply waited until her mother left her alone before quietly getting out of bed and swiftly packing a hold-all with a few personal belongings, not forgetting the love of her life, Lulu, a doll she had had since she was six years old.

Thanks to the five hundred shillings prize money, as a relay of cocks crowed to announce dawn she had already paid off a taxi and was standing on the doorstep of her eldest sister Ujeni's villa on the outskirts of Timbuka, the country's capital city.

"Adela! What brings you here at this ungodly hour?" a sleepy Ujeni began. Then she noticed with alarm her younger sister's bruised and swollen face. "My God! Come in quickly. What on earth has happened to you?"

Sitting at the kitchen table, clasping a mug of hot tea more for comfort than sustenance, Adela again wept as she told her story. Ujeni listened impassively. When at last her sister's voice trailed off into an embarrassed silence, she said, "I've been wondering how long it would be before it was your turn. I suppose that hearing you had won a beauty contest set the old goat off."

Adela stared unbelievingly at her. "You mean I'm not the first it has happened to?"

Ujeni gave a cynical laugh. "You were too young to know what went on in that God-fearing family home of ours. Maria, Estella, Salomi and me — we all went through it until Jamesi realised something was wrong . . . " Jamesi was the first born, coming before Ujeni. ". . . Jamesi threatened that dirty old man who happened to be our father with the clan elders and the police, so we were more or less safe while he was around. Now you know why we all rushed into marriage with whomsoever we wanted, without bothering to get father's blessing or approval. With Jamesi threatening to report him for incest if he made any trouble, the old man was in no position to raise objections."

Adela shuddered and sipped her tea. "I would never have guessed. What I don't understand is that he recently started beating me for the smallest thing. It's as though he finds the sight of me unbearable. Mother says he is being strict because he is worried about the dangers surrounding young girls these days."

Ujeni snorted with laughter. "He beat you as a means of trying to control his own unnatural urges! That's what I think. And he is the last man to talk about danger to young girls, because he is one of the biggest dangers around! As for our mother, surely you realise that she's terrified of him? She has always known what he was up to, but has been too scared to speak out about it."

"Well, neither have you, Maria, Estella or Salomi, spoken out about it," Adela pointedly said.

Ujeni raised her finely-plucked eyebrows a fraction. "We kept quiet for mother's sake, and that's why we all visit her and father and behave as though everything is normal between us."

Pouring more tea in order to avoid Adela's eyes, she added, "It's time you knew that before the AIDS scare our father was notorious for his womanising in Timbuka. We probably have half-brothers and sisters all over the place. Then the AIDS scare came along. Heaven alone knows where he and a lot of other silly old men got the idea that they could escape the AIDS epidemic if they confined themselves to virgins — although most of those old idiots must have already been HIV positive before embarking on their deflowering routine. In father's case, he must have thought he had it made, after looking around and realising that he had four virgins in his own house."

These terrible revelations concerning her own father filled Adela with an even deeper misery. "What makes men behave like that?" she asked plaintively. "You know, father wasn't the only one to frighten me. I didn't tell you that after the beauty contest, some of the boys who have known me and Keti since we were small waited for us outside the community hall, but instead of teasing and tormenting us as they usually do, they were suddenly pretending to be friendly in the oddest way and it seemed that they couldn't keep their hands off us. It made us feel dirty. We had to run to get away from them."

"It's the nature of the beast," Ujeni said. "My guess is that seeing you and Keti parading in that contest gave those boys the idea that you were no longer kids. They suddenly saw both of you as sex objects. I suppose they have all reached puberty, and I understand from Sam . . . " Sam was Ujeni's doctor husband. ". . . that for boys it is a more difficult time than it is for girls. It's not surprising that they tried to paw you. They were probably giving in to an instinct that was more baffling to them than it was to you and Keti."

"It's disgusting!" Adela exclaimed.

"It may be disgusting, but the fact remains that it is all part of growing up. In the case of some boys it seems to produce a sort of persuasive charm that they never had before, which is probably why so many girls of your age are talked into having sex before understanding the full implications. Sam is crusading for you youngsters to be taught that what you often believe to be love, is in fact the behaviour of certain glands," Ujeni said with a smile. "He believes that a practical, biological approach is the solution. I don't agree with him, because he has overlooked that very funny thing known as human nature. Anyway, to change the subject, you won't be going back to the old family home. You can stay with Sam and me. I will drive you to school every day and pick you up afterwards. Sam can spell things out to our parents. He is well aware of the problem with father. I told him everything before we were married."

Seeing Adela stifle a yawn, Ujeni led her to the guest room and saw her into bed.

"Get some rest," she advised. "You are taking a few days away from school because you'll cause a scandal if you arrive at St. Mary's High with your face looking as though you have fought ten rounds with Mohammed Ali!"

Adela managed a smile and then fell asleep. It was good to have a big sister who so easily took control of things.

Chapter 2

Adela must have slept for only a couple of hours before the strong morning sunlight pierced through a gap in the hastily-drawn curtains and shone directly upon her face. She opened her eyes slowly, and wondered where she was and what she was doing there. Then with an almost physical jolt, the events of the previous evening came flooding back and she stiffened at the memory. She flew out of bed to examine her face in the dressing-table mirror, and gasped at the sight of the damage inflicted by her father. The dull ache where he had kicked her ribs reminded her that she had been fortunate to escape worse injury, and she thanked God that she had the protection of Ujeni and Sam.

Ujeni, in her usual methodical fashion, wasted no time in informing the school that her sister was suffering a bout of fever, and would be staying at her home until she was better. Thanks to Sam's professional skill, Adela's injuries were soon less painful and no longer noticeably disfiguring, and after three days of lazing around the house, she was able to return to St. Mary's High.

Her schoolmates greeted her with good humoured jokes relative to her role as a beauty queen, but their high-spirited welcome was spoilt by a terse command from the elderly headmistress, Sr. Felicia, for Adela to present herself immediately in the school's office.

The tone of the interview was set as soon as Adela tapped on the door and was invited in. Sr. Felicia showed no interest in Adela's health. She straightaway demanded to know whether or not it was true that a pupil of St. Mary's High School had been sufficiently immodest as to enter a so-called beauty contest: and she pronounced the word 'beauty' with the utmost contempt.

Adela stammered as she tried to explain that the contest had not been as vile as the headmistress plainly imagined, saying, "We only entered it as a favour to the organiser, Sister. He was short of contestants and . . ."

Sr. Felicia blinked and broke in with "Am I to understand that you are not the only St. Mary's girl to have paraded in front of a crowd of . . . of men?"

Realising that there was a danger of involving Keti, Adela secretly crossed her fingers and replied, "I'm talking about myself and a friend of mine who is here to visit some neighbours."

The headmistress accepted the story, and continued. "Well, young woman, I hope you understand the damage you have inflicted on this highly-respected school. Your vain and thoughtless action has made a mockery of everything that St. Mary's has hitherto stood for — namely virtue, modesty and self-respect. We who are privileged to serve here have always prided ourselves on producing women who are good conscientious workers in their chosen professions, women who will eventually become excellent wives and mothers. In other words, women who are a credit to their church, community and country."

Adela made another attempt at defending herself, only to be silenced by Sr. Felicia's insistent monologue.

"Girls who believe that their physical attractions are more important than the purity of their souls can only be classed as vain and shallow — and there is no place for such girls in St. Mary's High school!"

"Oh, no!" Adela breathed, feeling that she was taking part in a totally unreal scene.

"Oh, yes!" Sr. Felicia rose like a gaunt bird of prey from behind the desk. "Your parents are being requested to remove you immediately, so clear your locker in the cloakroom, and report to matron. Wait with her until your parents arrive to collect you.

"I decided not to call them until I had assessed your attitude. I am saddened to see that you are not in the least repentant."

"But, Sister, I've done nothing wrong!" Adela cried.

Sr. Felicia's mouth twisted into a scornful smile. "That's what I mean by your unrepentance. Now you are free to go."

"Oh yes!" Sr. Felicia rose like a gaunt bird of prey from behind the desk

Adela stumbled to the door, turned and said in a voice choked with tears, "Please, Sister, I'm staying with my sister Ujeni and her husband. Will you be kind enough to call her to collect me?"

The headmistress abruptly agreed, and Adela wrote Ujeni's telephone number on a notepad. But she was distressed to hear that her parents would still have to be present at her formal dismissal from school.

It so happened that the parents and Ujeni arrived at the school within minutes of each other. The parents meekly accepted the headmistress's harsh ruling, but Ujeni refused to go down without a fight. She turned on Sr. Felicia with, "How can you expel my sister for entering and winning a silly beauty contest? You should be proud instead of affronted that she proved that St. Mary's girls have looks as well as brains? Really, Sister, are you asking us to believe that you prefer your pupils to resemble that back ends of cows?"

"How dare you speak to me like that!" the headmistress bleated, clutching as if for courage, at the wooden cross adorning her flat bosom. "It's common knowledge that beauty contests attract a very inferior type of girl. You only need to read the newspapers to realise that!"

Ujeni's eyes narrowed dangerously and she said, "Who would have believed that you ladies in Holy Orders are so familiar with the gutter Press? However, Sister, if you're inferring that my sister is a very inferior type of girl, perhaps you'll be prepared to verify your opinion in court — where you might find yourself defending a case of defamation of character!"

The headmistress sank back in her chair, and for the first time since confronting Adela's parents and Ujeni showed signs of unease.

"That's not at all what I meant," she muttered.

"Well, what did you mean?" Ujeni relentlessly pressed her. "Come on, Sister. You want to throw Adela out of school for what most reasonable folk would consider a girlish escapade, just before she is to sit for an important exam, and from what you have said, you are determined to leave the child without a shred of character." She glanced at the parents and added, "I think we have grounds for legal action here."

Sr. Felicia pulled herself together. "I can assure you that the Archbishop, who as you are aware is chairman of our board of governors, will undoubtedly back my decision concerning your sister. He and the other governors have very strict views on how our girls should behave both at school and in public.

"However, if you quietly remove Adela, I am willing to provide a testimonial as to her academic ability and general demeanour, which I can confirm was acceptable until she decided to be a so-called beauty queen."

Ujeni appeared to give the headmistress's suggestion some thought before saying, "Very well. We will take my sister away from St. Mary's and we'll accept your testimonial, provided that it is what we consider an honest assessment. But on condition that you explain Adela's leaving as our arranging for her to have specialised tutoring to ensure that she passes her exam."

"Such an excuse will not reflect well on our teaching methods," the headmistress protested.

"Take it or leave it," Ujeni told her. "Because if I hear the word 'expelled' as much as whispered in connection with my sister's leaving this school, I'll drag you and your board of governors through the courts and make you all the laughing stock of the country! The gutter Press that you nuns seem to find so interesting will have fun covering the story!"

While Ujeni and the headmistress wrangled, the parents had sat in miserable silence, and Adela had stared fixedly at the floor. Now, as she and Ujeni gathered up her books and personal belongings, and stowed them in the car, tears splashed down her cheeks. She found it unbearable to hear for the last time the soft buzz of normal school activity issuing from the open windows of classrooms.

"You can stop feeling sentimental," Ujeni sharply said to her. "See it as the end of one phase of your life, and the beginning of something new. You had better say goodbye to father and mother."

"Wouldn't it be better if she came home with us?" her mother timidly suggested.

"No, it would not," Ujeni snapped, glaring meaningfully at her father who bit his lip and hung his head.

"Well, at least let us know what you intend to do about her studies," the mother almost pleaded.

Ujeni softened. "Don't worry, mother. I'll make sure that Adela phones you every week, and as soon as she settles to home tutoring, you can spend a few days with us."

She started the car with a defiant roar, and Adela's last glimpse of her parents was of two forlorn people standing outside the main door of St. Mary's High School, looking as though they were unsure of what to do next.

Chapter 3

Not everybody was looking or feeling as hesitant as Adela's and Ujeni's parents. Yoweri Wamala, for instance, was fully confident about his future — and this showed in the squaring of his shoulders, the constant grin on his face, as well as the jauntiness in his step. Since his encounter with Joe Banda, life had definitely taken a turn for the better. Joe, it transpired, was everything Yoweri had always wanted to be: a man with connections in big business circles; somebody with the money to monopolise the national entertainment industry to the extent of importing the best of Africa's performers from as far afield as Nigeria and South Africa.

"Believe me, there's real money in the Beauty Queen racket," he had confided to Yoweri over drinks at the Zebra bar on the night of the Kabongo contest. "The people who run the Miss World competition are on to a goldmine, and anybody who can afford to groom a good-looking girl to their acceptable standard can make pots of money, even if the girl doesn't win."

"How?" Yoweri had wanted to know.

Joe's superior smirk secretly annoyed him, but he had listened intently to the man's explanation of sponsorships by local and international commercial organisations providing everything from cosmetics to limousines and overseas travelling expenses, not to mention the high fees paid for promoting various products.

"Those little contests of yours will never get anywhere, not the way you run them at present," was one of Joe's candid opinions that increased Yoweri irritation, although he appreciated that he was receiving valuable guidance from an experienced business tycoon and was determined to make the most of it. So he gave him his undivided attention as Joe went on to reveal how he had witnessed three of Yoweri's rough contests.

"Where you go wrong," Joe pointed out, "is first . . ." he began ticking off Yoweri's mistakes on his fingers" . . . not getting the local councils interested, and getting some local VIPs as guests of honour. Secondly, you don't have enough publicity. A few handwritten posters stuck up here and there around a township are hardly worth bothering about. You ought to have a set of professionally designed, eye-catching posters with blank spaces for you to fill in the different dates and venues. Thirdly, the entrants to the contest should enrol well in advance — that gives them time to pretty themselves up and get something really special to wear. This last minute habit of yours of having to practically drag young women off the street is disastrous. Twice I've watched you trying to persuade bar-girls to take part, and tonight I overheard you begging those two youngsters to do you a favour by entering your contest." Joe laughed drily and shook his head. "Mind you, it didn't surprise me that one of those youngsters turned out to be the winner. That girl has both style and class, Yoweri, whereas most of your other contestants had as much appeal as a broken-down bus."

As Yoweri attempted to make a comment, Joe stopped him with, "Let me finish. I can think of many more improvements you could make to the way you operate, but we'll leave them for the moment, because the fourth important criticism I have is the absence of a panel of judges. Has it never occurred to you that you would have ready-made, free publicity if you invited, say three or maybe six people from the glamour industry — folk from the top cosmetic manufacturers, high-class clothing boutiques, visiting celebrities?"

Yoweri was completely out of his depth. He muttered, "I could never afford such people."

Joe clapped him on the shoulder, nearly causing him to choke on his drink. "They wouldn't cost you a cent, and their public relations departments would attend to photographs and write-ups in the newspapers."

"I see what you mean," Yoweri doubtfully acknowledged.

"I don't think you do," Joe went on. "Allowing a crowd of semi-rural peasants to choose a beauty queen by the loudness and length of their applause is plain stupid. I've been secretly monitoring your contests, and you surely recall the one you held in Bakenda? The girl who won it just missed being completely ugly. Yet because the hall was packed solid with her clansmen, the other prettier contestants didn't stand a chance."

Yoweri remembered Bakenda, and a shiver ran down his spine. Thanks to the irate indignation of some of the other contestants' relatives who had been grossly outnumbered in the audience, he had been compelled to run for his life, leaving behind the original impressively carved throne (acquired cheaply at the auctioning of a deceased Asian's household goods), not to mention the rhinestone tiara which the winner had flatly refused to hand back to him.

Now he began wondering whether or not Joe Banda had invited him for a drink simply to tear to shreds his organisational skills, and he was toying with the idea of thanking Joe for his hospitality and leaving the Zebra bar immediately. But Joe suddenly lowered his voice and said "I've taken a lot of trouble to point out your mistakes in the hope that you are prepared to do things my way. Because if things work out as I want them to, there'll be a very good job for you in my outfit."

Yoweri nodded eagerly, gripped by excitement as Joe continued.

"That Miss Kabongo District. My instinct, and it's seldom wrong, tells me that we have an international winner there, if we play our cards right. Of course, it will take time. We'll need to put her in the hands of a number of professionals to teach her how to dress, do her hair, her face, that sort of thing, as well as to develop her personality. A couple of years in the right hands, and we should have a goose that lays golden eggs. Now, where can we find her?"

Yoweri's thrilling glimpse of life at the top instantly withered to nothing as it came to him in a flash that he knew neither Miss Kabongo District's surname nor her address.

"You must have her details on the enrolment form," Joe urged noticing Yoweri's state of alarm.

Consternation also gripped him when he learned that enrolment for entry to a contest played no part in Yoweri's arrangements.

21

"You mean you don't keep details of your contestants?" he gasped. "That you have no record whatsoever of the girls who compete?"

"I work on a very tight budget," Yoweri weakly pointed out. "You know how it is . . ."

"No, I don't know how it is," Joe snapped. "And get this straight, my friend, I'm offering you a chance to make your mark in real show business, only I won't put up with inefficiency. If you want to learn the trade from me, find that girl and find her fast. When you do, leave the talking to me. Is that clear?"

Going home, Yoweri gradually allowed his injured pride to give way to a strong feeling that fate was smiling upon him. By the time he parked the pick-up outside his home, he was singing to himself. His newly-found optimism was stronger than ever when, next morning, he set out determined to find Miss Kabongo District.

Chapter 4

Entering Kabongo Township, Yoweri made straight for the bar from where he had obtained four of his contestants in the Miss Kabongo District beauty contest. Only one of the girls was there, and she returned his greeting with a marked lack of enthusiasm. However, she accepted his offer of a drink, and sullenly joined him at a table.

His request for Adela's full name and address met with an indifferent shrug, and Yoweri at first thought he had misheard the girl when she suggested he should try St. Mary's High School.

"What is she doing there — teaching?" he asked, conversationally.

The bar-girl gave him a cool glance. "Teaching? Don't be a fool — she's a student. She passes by here nearly everyday with a group of other girls, all of them wearing the St. Mary's uniform."

"But she can't be!" Yoweri spluttered.

The girl giggled. "Fooled you, did she? Some of those school kids look too grown-up for their own good."

"How old do you reckon she is?" he asked, and audibly gulped when his companion told him, "Oh, I'd say anything between fourteen and fifteen."

"Oh, she must be nearer eighteen," he said, voicing his own wishful thinking. "Yes, you only have to look at her to see that she's mature."

"Why don't you ask her?" the girl suggested. "St. Mary's is only five minutes walk from here."

Leaving the bar, and on his way to the school, Yoweri reflected on his own impression of Miss Kabongo District. Although he had been careful not to say so to Joe Banda, he considered her and her friend a couple of sparrows when compared with the other contestants, most of whom had embodied Yoweri's personal ideas of beauty contestants by appearing in brightly-coloured, clinging dresses, elaborate wigs and lavish make-up. However, Joe was a man with experience in these things, and Yoweri was prepared to go along with him.

At St. Mary's High School all seemed quiet. Then a bell clanged and girls of all shapes and sizes swarmed noisily through the open gateway to wander in groups in various directions.

Yoweri intercepted four girls who slowed down to peer at a letter being laughingly read aloud by one of them. "Excuse me, miss," he began, swallowing hard under the haughty stare of four pairs of eyes.

"Go away. We're not allowed to speak to strange men," the letter-reader said in a manner that left no room for argument. After this undignified encounter, Yoweri was reluctant to approach other students because those who had witnessed his embarrassment were tittering and nudging each other. He stood undecided as to what his next move should be. He certainly did not fancy approaching any of the nuns who could be seen moving serenely between the school buildings.

Then, like an answer to a prayer, his beauty queen's friend and runner-up in the contest emerged from a row of classrooms and walked slowly towards him. Even from a distance, Yoweri noted her troubled expression, but he pinned a friendly grin to his own face and said "Hello! Remember me?"

Keti scowled at him. "I remember you, all right. And I wish I had never set eyes on you."

"What do you mean?" he asked, looking puzzled. "I'm sorry if you're disappointed at not winning the contest. I can tell you confidentially that it was a toss-up between you and your friend. If I had had my way, you would have won."

"I'm not at all worried about your stupid contest," Keti almost spat at him. "It has caused nothing but trouble. Now, clear off. The last thing I want is to be seen talking to you."

"Hey!" Yoweri caught her arm as she turned away. "Just a minute, miss! All I wanted to ask you was where I can find your friend, Miss Kabongo District. I have good news for her!" Keti shook off his hand and flung him a look of acute dislike.

"Don't you dare go around calling Adela Miss Kabongo District! Her people came and took her away from school. The story is that she is to have special tuition for the exam. But I believe that her leaving has something to do with your rotten beauty contest."

Keti, once started, could not stop herself from saying what had been milling around in her head ever since Adela had disappeared. "She never mentioned special tuition to me, and we tell each other everything. And then to go off with her elder sister without a word of goodbye!"

Yoweri was stunned. "Gone off with her sister?" he echoed. "To where?"

"How should I know?" Keti cried. She again began walking away, and he got into step beside her.

"Listen," he said, "It's very important that I find her. A friend of mine wants to talk to her and . . . "

"Will you please go away and leave me alone?" Keti angrily shouted at him. "Adela and I are not interested in sugar daddies."

"It's nothing like that," Yoweri assured her desperately. "Honestly, this friend of mine is a highly-respected businessman, and he's offering your friend the chance of a very profitable career. Don't you think that she is entitled to at least hear what it is he is offering, and make up her own mind about accepting or turning it down?"

"Well, I've already told you that I have no idea where she is, so you'd better make your enquiries somewhere else."

Yoweri refused to give up. He said

"You must know where her parents live. Couldn't you find out from them?"

"I could, but I won't," Keti flatly declared.

Yoweri decided to soften his approach. "I'm sorry if you think my beauty contest was responsible for your friend leaving school so suddenly," he said. "Although I can't understand how the two happenings are connected, if you could find out where she is, there's no reason why you shouldn't come with me and my friend when we go to talk to her. That way, you would soon find out that everything is above board, and that my beauty contest couldn't possibly be responsible for Adela leaving the school."

Keti was still not convinced that the beauty contest had no bearing on Adela's swift removal from St. Mary's High. The headmistress, Sr. Felicia was known for her obsession with modesty: she had once expelled a prize pupil for carrying lipstick in her school satchel; and St. Mary's netball team, at her insistence, played in voluminous skirts and thick undergarments rather than the trim shorts worn by all their opponents. Keti wondered how she herself had escaped the wrath of the narrow-minded nun.

Nonetheless, she was anxious to know exactly what had happened to her best friend, if only to scotch the rumour flying around the school that Adela was pregnant.

"Right," she eventually said to Yoweri, much to his relief. "I'll speak to Adela's parents. I have to return a couple of her textbooks anyway."

Yoweri was all for accompanying her on her mission, but she firmly made him wait at a kiosk that sold tea near a busy bus stop.

At the home of Adela's parents, Keti was reluctantly invited inside, and an uncomfortable silence developed as soon as the usual greetings were exchanged. In handing over the borrowed books, Keti expressed mild surprise that Adela had left the school without saying goodbye to any of her classmates.

"Yes, it was rather sudden," Adela's mother nervously agreed. "Ujeni, our eldest daughter, and her husband, Sam, arranged the special tuition, so we all had to fit into their plan."

Adela's father grunted something about it being time for Keti to be on her way, that it was not safe for young girls to walk alone after sunset, and although sunset was two hours away, Keti took the hint and got up to leave. At the door, she paused.

26

"Could I possibly have Adela's address, or maybe a phone number where I can reach her? I would like to keep in touch."

Despite a furious warning frown from her husband, Adela's mother replied,

"Of course, child. I'll give you Ujeni's number. Do you have something to write it on? If you want to send her a letter, let me have it by the weekend, because I shall be spending a few days with them next week."

A few minutes later, as Keti walked down the verandah steps with the phone number tucked in her blouse pocket, she was aware of raised voices coming from the house, and distinctly heard Adela's mother argue,

"I will not have a child of mine treated like a leper! She is entitled to keep her friends, no matter what she has done!"

This left Keti with the disquieting impression that the rumour of pregnancy might not be totally unfounded although she was forced to admit that the Adela she knew seemed stuck at the stage of being more interested in dolls than in members of the opposite sex.

Yoweri's face broke into a wide smile as soon as he saw Keti coming towards him. He had been worried sick that she may have taken it into her head to simply dump him.

"Well, have you got Adela's new address?" he demanded.

"I've got a phone number," Keti said, "and I'm not passing it on to you until I've spoken to Adela and she agrees to meet you and your friend."

Yoweri argued but Keti refused to hand over the phone number. He had to be content to stand outside the phone booth while she made the call.

Ujeni answered promptly, although she was reluctant to put her younger sister on the line.

"Yes, Adela is here," she cautiously admitted. "May I ask who wants to speak to her?"

27

[Keti]... *again began walking away, and he got into step beside her.*

"Will you tell her that it's Keti from school? Your mother gave me this number when I called at the house to return some of Adela's books."

"Oh. Hold on a minute."

Before Adela came to the phone, Ujeni could be heard reminding her to 'stick to the story', then came Adela's excited voice.

"Keti! Is it really you?"

"It's me, all right!" Keti laughed. "What do you mean by running off without as much as a Cheerio or See You Soon?"

"Oh, sorry about that . . ."

Keti noticed how Adela suddenly sounded strangely false. "I suppose mother told you that Ujeni and Sam are insisting that I have private tuition to make sure I pass the exam in my weakest subjects? I intended to write you a note as soon as I settled in here."

Keti had the uncomfortable feeling that Ujeni was standing close to Adela, doing her best to hear every word that was said, and she was also puzzled that Ujeni and her husband should suddenly be in charge of her friend's education. Nevertheless, she went ahead and told Adela about the beauty contest organiser's reappearance, and passed on the message concerning his business associate.

"What can he possibly want?" Adela wondered aloud. "I don't think I want anything to do with that contest organiser or his pal. The biggest mistake I ever made was to let that man persuade me to . . ."

The phone was snatched out of Adela's hand, and Ujeni barked, "I don't know what this is about, but tell that beauty contest man to leave my sister alone, or I'll kill him! And you, young woman, if you have nothing better to do than try to involve my sister with sugar daddies, please do not call my house again!"

The receiver was slammed down, and, at her end of the line, Keti was left with the impersonal hum of the dialling tone.

"Well, did you manage to fix up a meeting?" Yoweri asked her as she stumbled miserably from the booth.

Keti shook her head. "Go away. Because of you, I've lost my best friend!"

With that, she fled blindly down the road. In her haste to get as far away as possible from Yoweri, she failed to notice that the scrap of paper bearing Ujeni's phone number had slipped from her fingers and now lay on the floor of the phone booth. Yoweri spotted it and immediately pocketed it. After seeing the shattering effect that a call to that particular number had had on Keti, he was not anxious to undergo the same experience.

"Joe Banda can handle this," he decided. "At least he can't accuse me of coming back empty-handed."

Chapter 5

Joe Banda won Yoweri's grudging admiration by the way he handled things with the minimum of information at hand. The telephone number alone enabled him to trace the physical address of Ujeni and Sam, which he did by having a few words with one of his contacts, a senior executive in Mantola Posts and Telecommunications. Yoweri was greatly impressed by the speed with which Joe's request was granted. But then everything about Joe was impressive, Yoweri was forced to acknowledge as he lounged in an easy chair upholstered in real leather, doing his utmost to look as though frequenting office suites as sumptuous as Joe's was something he did everyday. Someday, he told himself, I shall be the expensively-suited man behind the massive polished desk: I shall be the man with the network of influential friends.

He had been slightly nervous about letting Joe know that Adela was only fourteen years old. Joe, however, was not in the least flustered by the news.

"Fourteen, you say? Well, maybe that's a good thing. It means that we can mould her to our own design. Her age gives us a better chance of having her ready within two years, and then we shall simply provide her with a birth certificate that bumps her age up."

"Supposing she and her family refuse to go along with your — our plans!" Yoweri tentatively remarked.

Joe laughed cynically. "Nobody will dream of refusing as soon as they hear how much money we're talking about."

A few hours later, leaving Yoweri to read a collection of reports on beauty competitions from all over the world, he parked his car outside Ujeni's and Sam's house. A maid opened the door, and Joe, flourishing a briefcase, informed her that he would like to speak to the householder. As he intended, the girl was overwhelmed by his air of officialdom and rushed indoors to return after a moment or two with Ujeni.

31

... Ujeni suspiciously eyed the gleaming limousine and Joe's prosperous appearance.

"Yes, what can I do for you?"

As she addressed him, Ujeni suspiciously eyed the gleaming limousine and Joe's prosperous appearance. He smiled charmingly.

"Would it be possible to have a private word with you, madam? The subject is rather delicate."

"Are you by any chance from the Department of Inland Revenue?" she asked, remembering something that Sam had said about government inspectors tracking down tax-dodgers. Joe laughed heartily, showing gleaming teeth.

"Good heavens, whatever gave you that idea? I hope that I don't strike you as so intimidating?"

Ujeni joined in the laughter, more from the relief than amusement, and impulsively invited him in for coffee. While waiting for the arrival of the coffee, and as they were seated in an airy sitting-room opening onto the garden, Joe endeared himself to his hostess by complimenting her on her good taste in home decor and the serene atmosphere she had created.

"In my experience, only very intelligent women are successful in creating a truly relaxing background to domestic life," he said. "Your husband is extremely fortunate."

Joe's eyes twinkled, as he mischievously added, "Although I don't suppose he thought so when he was handed the bills for all this exclusive furnishing!"

Ujeni gave him a conspirator's wink. She was delighted with this amusing stranger. A boring afternoon was turning into a pleasant social occasion.

"Oh, you men!" she giggled. "You always complain about money spent on the home, yet it is only for your own benefit. My husband may grumble at the expense, but I know that he would be impossible to live with without his creature comforts!"

Joe sighed. "How well I know what you mean. I must confess that I, too, would be most unhappy if I didn't have a well-run, comfortable home. I don't care what happens so long as my home remains stable, and my family and I continue our comfortable life-style."

The maid brought the coffee, and as Ujeni poured, he said "I consider myself very fortunate. So many Matolans are struggling to make ends meet. Not . . ." he hastily added, "that we are the only African country in this position. I assure you, conditions are far worse not a million miles from our borders. But then, dear lady, I'm sure you are well-acquainted with how world recession affects us all, not to mention what countries have to do to qualify for World Bank and IMF support. My sympathy lies with the younger generations.

I really feel for all those youngsters who work hard for exams and university degrees, and at the end of all their hard work we can offer them nothing. Absolutely nothing!"

Ujeni quickly jumped in with "I couldn't agree more. The world is indeed a sorry mess!"

The truth was that she was enchanted to have her imposing visitor discussing what she considered to be world affairs with her in the belief that she was capable of understanding what he was talking about. It was a long time since her husband, Sam, had credited her with a brain. Sam, an overworked doctor in a lucrative private practice, was usually too tired to do more than eat a meal before falling asleep in front of the television. His conversations with Ujeni were generally confined to basic domestic issues, and/or arguments concerning the way she spent his money.

Joe continued to weave his spell by asking Ujeni for her views on various topics, and listening to her answers as though they were of importance to him.

He took her by surprise when, after hearing her opinion of the professional politicians who had been quick to jump on the Women's Rights bandwagon, he suddenly said, "You and I could go on all day chatting like old friends. Aren't you curious to know what brings me here?"

She laughed nervously. "Why, of course! Do tell me."

Joe opened his briefcase and took out a glossy folder. "I want you to look at these," he explained, handing the folder to her.

Puzzled, she examined the press-cuttings and glossy photographs of glamorous girls from all over Africa, some elegant in national costume, others in skimpy swimsuits.

"What have these to do with me?" she asked him.

Joe gazed frankly into her eyes. "If my information is correct, you are presently housing a young woman who could, with the correct handling, make these . . ." he flicked a contemptuous finger at the posing beauties," look like yesterday's stale plantain!"

"You . . . you mean Adela?" Ujeni faltered. Then, with more spirit, "Sorry to waste your time, sir, but this sort of business is no good to her. She's preparing for an important exam. Besides, she's only fourteen years old."

"Don't be hasty." Joe placed a well-manicured hand on her bare arm, and she found his touch disturbingly pleasant. "Only three of the girls you see here made it to the Miss World competition." He tightened his grip on her arm. "I am willing to place my personal reputation on the line in guaranteeing that your sister has a golden future in the beauty competition business. Have you any idea how much these beauty queens can earn?"

Without waiting for Ujeni to hazard a guess, he turned the pages of the folder until he came to a picture of a lithesome girl wearing a leopard skin swimsuit. "This is a girl from Vendiza. Take a good look at her. She never made it to the Miss World contest, yet she and her manager raked in a conservative quarter of a million US dollars."

"How much?" Ujeni croaked.

"You heard me. She was sponsored by a number of international companies and several influential black American organisations who were determined to have a black, preferably African, Miss World. Advertising campaigns for various cosmetics, perfumes and clothes must have brought in most of her earnings. It was her sponsors' tough luck that the girl got pregnant and hid it from everybody until it was too late for anything to be done about it or for them to groom a replacement."

Ujeni was fascinated. "What makes you think that my sister could succeed where so many others have failed?" she asked.

Joe removed his fingers from her arm and took her hand, and again she enjoyed the sensation. He said, "I have a very strong instinct in these matters. I have an account with an overseas firm whose business it is to place bets on everything from horse racing to the outcome of general elections in different parts of the world. In other words, I gamble on a big scale — and over the past few years I have made notable amounts of money by gambling on the Miss World competition. I picked the winner everytime!"

"What do you call a notable amount?" Ujeni shrewdly wanted to know.

"Oh, anything upwards of thirty thousand US dollars."

She blinked as if to convince herself that this conversation was really taking place, and that she was not dreaming.

"Thirty thousand US dollars?" she whispered.

Joe nodded complacently, waiting for her to say something more.

"But I've told you my sister is only fourteen years old. I should imagine that she is far too young to enter any important contest. From what you say, I gather that you had something to do with the Miss Kabongo District fiasco — and I must make it clear that that was a very silly mistake from Adela's point of view."

Joe Banda quickly assured her that the Miss Kabongo District affair was in no way connected with him, although he admitted that his interest in Adela had arisen from that particular competition. As for Adela's tender years, he said airily, "That's something we can work on. This venture is much too important to be ruined by trying to rush things. As I see it, we'll need about two years to streamline your sister above and beyond the usual international beauty standards. She already has a very special quality. It's our job to make the most of it."

Ujeni noticed his use of 'we' in place of 'I', and realised that this man who had so far not introduced himself was taking it for granted that she was ready to fall in with his plans. She experienced a twinge of guilt at allowing the idea of pots of money to override the sisterly concern and protection that she was supposed to be providing for Adela. But she was also quick to reason that Adela was no intellectual genius: that she was destined to join the ranks of the unemployed unless a miracle happened. A lucrative future as a beauty queen under the guidance of somebody so obviously successful as this impressive stranger was undoubtedly infinitely preferable, and Ujeni convinced herself that Adela would agree with her on this.

Joe was good at reading other people's minds, and he knew how to manipulate them into believing that they were doing the right thing by falling in with his plans. He said, "Of course, there is every reason for the young lady to complete her studies. Beauty and brains, eh? I understand that you are arranging special tuition? I like that. Presumably her studies are part-time, in which case she will be able to attend a charm school that someone I know has recently opened in Timbuka. Maxi, the lady who owns this place, is a qualified beautician and once worked as a model in New York. I think Adela will enjoy her classes." Having watched Ujeni wrestle with her conscience, he continued, "Your sister will have cause to be very grateful to you when she is heading for fame and fortune, and her poor contemporaries are queuing for too few miserable, underpaid jobs."

Ujeni, partly reassured by his bland words, voiced the questions that had been on the tip of her tongue ever since the subject of Adela as a potential Miss World had been broached. "How do you know so much of what is going on in our family?"

"Oh, my dear lady!" Joe chuckled, producing a business card from his wallet, "this should give you some idea of my interests. As you see, I'm in the entertainment industry. It's part of my job to spot talent. As

37

for your family affairs, well, I learnt the little I know after I employed a young man who . . . er . . . I was going to say 'organised', but perhaps 'managed' describes his pathetic operation better . . . yes, a young man who managed the beauty contest won by Adela. He talked to one of Adela's schoolfriends, and I tracked you down from the telephone number given to that young friend by your parents."

"I see," Ujeni murmured: only she didn't, not really. "Who would be paying for the charm school and the other expenses sure to arise in turning my sister into a beauty queen?"

"Don't you worry your pretty little head about that!" Joe retorted. "As the chief shareholder in the limited company we shall form to promote Adela, I will be responsible for all immediate capital outlay. I'm perfectly confident of a good return on my investment."

"Well, Mr. Banda . . ." Ujeni began.

"Please call me Joe."

"All right, Joe. I find your proposal very appealing, especially if my husband and I are allowed shares in the company, but I mustn't give a final commitment until I have talked it over with my husband and, of course, Adela."

"You and your husband will certainly have a block of shares in the company — and you personally will be entitled to chaperoning fees as soon as we reach the stage of entering Adela for beauty contests. It is most important that not a hint of scandal or inappropriate behaviour touches our star! For take my word for it, a star your sister is destined to be. From the Beauty Queen circuit, it's a short and easy step to the American movies."

As Ujeni's imagination roamed excitedly in the direction of Hollywood and rubbing shoulders with world celebrities, Joe broke into her dream with, "I'm glad that you wish to delay the final decision until you have consulted your husband. I like to know that I'm dealing with a family team. My phone number is on the business card I gave you. Please call me as soon as you come to a decision, or if you have any queries. Incidentally, I've given my bank manager permission to release any information you may require regarding my financial status. Let me have the card and I'll write his private office number on the back."

Shortly after supplying his bank manager's phone number, Joe made his farewells. As soon as his car was out sight, Ujeni telephoned Sam at his clinic. "Try to get home earlier than usual," she told him. "Something fantastic has happened, Sam. We must talk!"

Sam, in the middle of examining an elderly patient showing typical signs of defective kidneys, was irritated at the interruption. "How often do I have to tell you not to call me here unless it is an emergency!" he barked.

"This is just as important as an emergency," Ujeni replied. "If we handle it properly, our lives will change for the better!"

She barely had time to replace the receiver before Adela entered the room. Ujeni stared at her younger sister as if seeing her for the first time, trying to detect that special quality that Joe Banda insisted was there. And what did she see? She saw a young girl, tall for her age, with slender, tapering limbs and a graceful length of neck. The delicate facial structure was not in the least remarkable in Ujeni's eyes, because it was characteristic of their mother's family and strongly evident in herself and her other siblings as much as in Adela.

'I must have looked just like that when I was fourteen years old,' Ujeni mused, wondering yet again what Joe Banda saw as so special.

"I'm bored!" Adela announced, flinging herself into the chair recently vacated by Joe.

"In that case, you'd better get down to your school books," Ujeni said, "Miss Girani, who lives up the road from here, is a retired headmistress and she is delighted at the idea of tutoring you. She is expecting you at her house by nine tomorrow morning."

"Are you saying that I'll be studying with her on my own?" Adela exclaimed. "I thought you said I'd be attending a private place called a 'crammer', where they prepare people for exams? There'll be no fun in studying on my own!"

Ujeni responded coolly. "As far as I remember, studying was never fun, whether or not I did it with other people. Anyway, you can stop sulking. You are going to Miss Girani. She is a competent old soul — and she needs the money."

Adela sank into utter dejection. She wished with all her heart that she and Keti had resisted the pleading of that wretched beauty contest organiser. Had they done so, the pair of them would at this moment be walking home from school, discussing the latest rumours and school gossip.

In defiance of Ujeni's instructions to take out her textbooks, Adela went to her room and dug out a Jackie Collins novel that had been doing the rounds at school for two whole terms. The main plot was in itself thrilling, but Adela, like most of her schoolmates, made little sense of some of the sexual antics indulged in by the main characters. At times, they quite turned her stomach, and almost persuaded her that, rather than face marriage and all that it apparently entailed, she would be more comfortable as a nun.

Deep in the adventures of a glamorous heroine, she heard Sam's car drive up to the house. She was vaguely aware that Sam was home earlier than usual, but she carried on reading. Only half-an-hour later, when raised voices coming from the sitting-room aroused her curiosity did she put aside the novel and wander off to find out what was going on.

She stopped in her tracks, in the square-tiled hallway, the moment she heard her name mentioned, afraid to accept that perhaps she was no longer welcome in Ujeni's and Sam's marital home.

Sam, she was relieved to hear, was the one defending her interests. After all, the house, as far as she knew, belonged to him. She heard him exclaim, "How can you even consider doing such a thing to your own flesh and blood? Adela has entrusted herself to our care. We are, to all intents and purposes, her guardians. I absolutely refuse to condone this plan between you and this . . . this Joe Banda, and I will do everything in my power to put a stop to it!"

Joe who? Adela did not recognise the name, and she was equally baffled when Ujeni talked of shares in a company, and Mr. Banda shouldering the expenses.

"I'm not listening to any more of this rubbish! And I'm certainly not interested in having shares in any company formed to treat that child as a marketable commodity!" Sam shouted. "I'm where I am, a respected and useful member of the community, I hope, through my own hard work, and I've no intention of trying to get filthy rich on the back of my youngest sister-in-law!"

He hurtled from the sitting-room with such force that he nearly collided with Adela. "Do you want to be a beauty queen, Adela?" he asked her, his eyebrows raised mockingly. "Do you want to expose yourself to cheap publicity exploiting your good looks? Take my advice. Attend to your books, child. Knowledge will stay with you long after everybody has forgotten how pretty you are."

"What was that all about?" Adela worriedly asked Ujeni, as soon as Sam strode furiously into his study, and she had run into the sitting-room to confront her sister.

Ujeni decided that there was nothing to lose by revealing Joe Banda's proposition, so she pulled Adela down on the sofa and sat close to her. Then she proceeded to recount what Joe had in mind.

"Oh, no!" Adela sprang to her feet and violently shook her head. "I've had enough of beauty contests. I'd still be in school with Ketĭ but for that silly man talking us into entering his rotten competition. Never again will I parade myself in front of a mob of yobbos!"

"But don't you see? It wouldn't be like that," Ujeni argued. "Mr. Banda is in a totally different class from the organiser you were unfortunate to meet. He would never dream of having you appear in some dreary community hall with a bunch of bar girls. Mr. Banda is talking about London, Paris and New York. He's talking about making you rich and famous. Why, he's ready to gamble everything he owns on your being crowned Miss World one day!"

"I don't want to be Miss World!" wailed Adela.

"No!" Ujeni snapped, on the verge of losing her temper. "No. I suppose you'd rather plod on, getting mediocre results in exams, and then think yourself lucky to land a typing job in some cramped office where they can't afford to pay more than the minimum wage!"

Adela burst into tears and sank back on the sofa.

"There, there," her sister attempted to soothe her. "There's nothing to cry about. We only want what's best for you. We want to see you independent and happy, that's all. Mr. Banda is a good man, and he is offering you a wonderful opportunity."

"I want to see my friend Keti," Adela sobbed.

Ujeni smiled. "Why not? How will it be if we invite her here for the weekend?"

"Would you?" Adela's tears dried like magic. She sensed that she had the advantage. "And there's something else . . ."

"Yes? Come on. Tell me." Ujeni pressed her.

"It's Lulu — my doll. She needs some clean clothes."

Ujeni had a rare flash of insight into her younger sister's thinking. She vividly recalled the day Sam had flown back from the United States, not many months after they married, and the doll he brought for Adela. Adela's birth had caused consternation because at the time her mother was nearing fifty. From the word go, she was surrounded by adolescent and grown-up siblings. It was only natural that from the start she should be everybody's pet. And it was no wonder that she remained a child in what was rapidly becoming a woman's body. Looking at Adela's development objectively, Ujeni suddenly understood that this sister of hers had never been allowed to grow up. She was petted and pampered, and she had clung to the doll, named Lulu, long after most girls of her age had stopped playing with dolls. Only a few weeks ago, Ujeni had come across Adela diligently sewing a new outfit for Lulu.

"I'll make sure that mother brings Lulu's clothes with her when she comes to stay with us next week," she promised.

As she made the promise, Ujeni instinctively realised what the special quality Joe Banda recognised in her sister was. It was innocence.

Chapter 6

Adela and Keti walked down the broad steps of the commercial building housing Maxi's Charm School and climbed into the back seat of Ujeni's car.

"How did it go?" Ujeni asked them, pulling away from the curb.

Adela wrinkled her nose. "Oh, I suppose it was all right, but it's becoming a bit of a bore. We experimented with the new Paris make-up, after we had gone through the aerobic routine."

Keti merely smiled. She had been unusually quiet all evening. The two girls had been attending Maxi's Charm School for the past two years. Joe Banda had suggested it and was paying both sets of fees after it became clear that Adela could make life difficult for everybody around her unless she had the regular company of someone of her own age. Ujeni had easily gained the consent of Keti's parents by telling them that poise and good grooming as well as academic qualifications were essential to any girl who hoped to find a decent job when she left school or university.

Of course, during the many weekends spent with Adela at Ujeni's and Sam's house, Keti very soon learned the truth about her friend's unexpected removal from St. Mary's High School, as well as the reason behind these lessons in deportment and beauty enhancement. Keti, sworn to secrecy by Ujeni, was careful not to mention any of this at school, and she also kept quiet about her own misgivings concerning the planning of Adela's future.

But nobody could overlook the striking transformation that had taken place in both girls since they began attending Maxi's classes. Maxi had taken two raw schoolgirls and turned them into elegant young women. Her emphasis was more on beauty through health, rather than through superficial beauty aids. So during the first year of two weekly lessons she concentrated on teaching the importance of a balanced diet, regular exercise, skin care, hair care, manicure and pedicure. One lesson each month was devoted to deportment, in which girls were taught how to walk, stand and sit with the utmost grace. Only in their second year at Maxi's were they introduced to the discreetly improving application of make-up and taught how to wear clothes and jewellery with good taste and impact.

Now, as Adela and Keti lounged comfortably yet decoratively, as they were taught, in Ujeni's car, on the way to Keti's home, they discussed the up-and-coming, all important university entrance exam.

"I shall have to miss Maxi's for a couple of weeks," Keti said. "If I don't start revision this weekend, I won't have any hope of passing."

"Adela will have to do some extra studying, too," Ujeni put in. "Miss Girani is not very optimistic about her chances in this exam, considering that she only just scraped through the last."

"We can always take the exam again," Adela petulantly pointed out. "Most students are eighteen before they sit for it."

"Yes, but you know at St. Mary's we are expected to use the years between leaving school and going to university to work on one of the Archbishop's charitable projects. That's why we take exams at an earlier age than most other schools." Keti said.

Adela scoffed petulantly. "What rubbish. You know as well as I do that Sr. Felicia only insists on it so that people will say how wonderful she is to get such young girls accepted for university! Nobody outside the school knows how she slave-drives her poor students. I mean, look at the amount of homework dished out in that place. You end up doing more studying at home than you do in the classroom!"

Keti turned her head and stared out of the window. She was still very fond of Adela, but more and more she suffered an uneasy feeling that her friend's pampered life-style was turning her into a mini-monster. Keti blamed Ujeni and Joe Banda for this state of affairs. The two of them treated Adela as though she were a fragile, precious object. Nothing was allowed to upset or even mildly dismay her, and, as far as Keti could see, she was refused nothing within reason, except the freedom to be like other teenage girls. The set-up puzzled Keti. Yes, she knew that her friend was being groomed as a beauty queen, and she knew that Adela was, according to Joe Banda, destined to earn lots of money. What she failed to understand was how much. Had she been aware of what was at stake, she might have appreciated that Ujeni and especially Joe Banda were only taking good care of their investment.

The fact remained, however, that Adela responded to their fuss and attention by growing increasingly outrageous in her demands, careless of other people's feelings, and disagreeably self-centred. There were times when Keti dreaded the weekends spent with her, and she was thankful for the excuse of studying for the exam that would relieve her for a while of any obligation to her friend.

Suddenly the car phone which Joe Banda had presented to Ujeni gave out it's subtle shrill signal of an incoming call, and Ujeni, to whom it was still of sufficient novelty, eagerly picked up the receiver and spoke a bright "Hello! Ujeni Kampare speaking from her car!"

The two listened with interest, saw her frown slightly, then heard her say, "Right, Joe. I'll do my best."

After replacing the receiver, she threw a swift glance over her shoulder at Keti and said, "Keti would you mind if we went straight back to our house, and took you home later? Something important has come up. Joe says it can't wait."

Keti, who had been looking forward to supper with her parents and her eldest brother visiting with his wife, tried to keep the disappointment out of her voice as she answered, "Of course not. Only I musn't stay to long."

"That's my girl!" Ujeni smiled at her in the driving mirror.

They arrived at the house and found Joe Banda and Yoweri Wamala waiting in the sitting-room. Sam's car stood in the drive, but he had disappeared into the study. Keti had long been aware that he did not approve of what was planned for his youngest sister-in-law.

Joe leapt to his feet as soon as they entered the room and clutched Ujeni's hand. "Great news!" he announced. "Before I spoke to you, I called Maxi. She believes we are ready to take off."

Ujeni dimpled at him. "Really, Joe! Couldn't this have waited? We were halfway to Keti's house when I got your call. And you did say that it was important."

Joe beamed at her, Adela and Keti. "It is important. Yoweri here discovered that Pan Africa Oil are staging a beauty contest at the Inter-Continental Hotel Nairobi next month. The prize is five thousand US dollars and an all expenses paid trip to Britain for the winner to feature in a promotion campaign. The entrants have to be registered by the day after tomorrow. Yoweri managed to get the forms delivered by DHL. Now all he needs is Adela's signature and one of those photos we took last week. He will fly to Kenya and deliver everything personally tomorrow morning."

Adela took the sheaf of forms that Yoweri was holding, and glanced through them. Then she looked up at Joe. "It says here that contestants must provide a copy of their birth certificate to prove they are eighteen years of age or over," she said questioningly.

With a flourish, Joe produced a certificate from the inner pocket of his jacket. "Here it is, Madam! I took the precaution of getting it some time ago. It proves conclusively that Adela is eighteen years of age."

"But I'm not!" Adela protested.

"You are now," Joe quietly told her. "And don't you ever forget it!"

For some reason she could not explain, Keti found his demeanour menacing. She glanced at Adela and recognised a flash of fear in her eyes.

Ujeni continued to study the registration forms. Her brow furrowed, and she eventually remarked, "Joe, isn't this rather like throwing her in at the deep end? This contest is open to girls from all over Africa, most of whom, I imagine, are already experienced in beauty competitions. I thought it was agreed that we would first try Adela out in some of the local contests?"

Joe's beaming smile widened, and he nodded. "That was the idea at first, but surely you can see that winning local contests will do nothing for her. Adela is way ahead of anything this whole country has to offer. Maxi agrees with me that Adela is ripe for the international scene. Besides, I'm ready to put my money where my mouth is. There's a betting shop in Nairobi that takes bets and pays out in hard currency. I'll prove my faith in Adela by gambling for five thousand US dollars — the equal of the prize being offered — on her winning the Pan Africa Oil competition!"

"Oh, Joe!" Ujeni put a hand to her throat as though about to faint.

"Now, come on, down to business," Joe briskly said. "Adela, you sign those forms while your sister and I plan the action!"

Keti watched Adela sign, and caught a glimpse of the birth certificate which added two years to Adela's age. Behind her, she could hear Joe and Ujeni arguing about the outfits Adela would need.

"Remember, the Press will probably meet the contestants as they arrive at the airport." Joe said.

"National costume," Ujeni decided. "Let it immediately be known where she comes from. I notice that Western evening dress is to be worn for the final line-up in the competition."

"That's so that they can see how well a girl will adjust to different styles of clothing," Joe explained. "Let's see that latest issue of *Vogue* magazine. Adela must have something really sensational. Maxi knows an excellent dressmaker — 'says the woman can copy anything . . .'"

Keti sank into a chair and wished with all her heart that she had been sufficiently strong-minded to insist upon being driven home. Across the room, Yoweri was apparently explaining how he had found out about the competition, which had not been given wide publicity in the Matola national press, since the country had little experience of beauty contests.

Then, as she was wondering whether or not Joe Banda would be generous enough to send her home in a taxi, instead of keeping her hanging around until Ujeni had time to drive her, Adela called out,

"Hey, Keti! You'll be coming with me to Nairobi! It says here that all contestants have to be accompanied by a chaperone!"

"That will be Ujeni's job," Joe briefly raised his head from *Vogue* magazine, then carried on discussing the intricacies of designer fashion with Ujeni.

"Oh, no it won't!" Adela rushed across the room and planted herself in front of him, hands on hips. "If Keti doesn't go, neither do I!"

Joe's usual good humour gave way to suppressed fury. He glared up at Adela and said, "It's time that you, young lady, got things clear. I'm the one who has prepared you for a fabulous future. It's my money that's changed you from an ordinary school kid into something special. So get it into that silly little head of yours that from now on what I say goes! Ujeni will be your chaperone, OK?"

Ujeni, realising that Adela was on the verge of tears, quickly put in "Oh, come on, Joe. Would it make much difference if all three of us travelled to Kenya?"

Joe turned on her with an expression she had never before seen on his face. "I'm going, you're going, Yoweri's going, Adela's going, Maxi's going. We don't have room for camp followers. Sorry Keti, but that's the way it is."

Keti felt bound to say something to ease the tense atmosphere. She had been waiting to break her own news to Adela when they were alone. Now seemed the right time, even though she would have preferred more privacy. "Please don't quarrel over me," she said. "I couldn't in any case have gone to Nairobi for the contest." She paused and looked nervously at Adela. "You see, I've already made up my mind to join a new order of nuns dedicated to the nursing of AIDS patients. If I pass my exams, I'll be accepted at their nurses' training centre instead of going to university, and they want me to work with them in my spare time to make sure that I'm joining them for all the right reasons."

"You're not going to be a nun!" Adela screamed. "You can't leave me!"

49

"I'm sorry, Adela. I have to," Keti said as she picked up her purse and walked to the door. "Is there any chance of someone calling a taxi?" she asked, amazed at her own quiet confidence.

"Let me run you home," Yoweri offered, escorting her from the house.

They both pretended not to hear Adela's hysterical ragings coming from the sitting-room as they drove away.

Two Weeks Later

Chapter 7

Adela, Ujeni, Maxi, Joe.Banda and Yoweri Wamala left for Nairobi quietly on a bright Tuesday morning.

The only well-wishers to see the party off were Adela's mother and her friend Keti, and both of them had been sworn to secrecy about the purpose of the journey. It must be said that neither looked very happy. Adela's mother dreaded the reaction of her husband and relatives when, as was certain to eventually happen, they learnt of her youngest daughter's launch into the beauty queen business. She herself was most uneasy and secretly ashamed about it. Being more of an age to be Adela's grandmother rather than her mother, she was conditioned to respect what the modern generation regarded as old-fashioned conventions, as were her own brothers and sisters, and her immediate in-laws. To her, there was something sinful in glorifying the body at the expense of the soul. But she was much too timid to speak her mind, and meekly accepted Ujeni and Joe Banda taking full control of Adela.

Her husband had even less to say on the subject. Strong condemnation for what he had tried to do to Adela — first by his eldest son, Jamesi, then by Ujeni's husband, Sam — had left the old man with no authority over any of his children. He had not set eyes on Adela since Ujeni had confided the sordid story to Joe Banda who had not hesitated to ban home visits by his protegee.

"I'm not taking any risks with my investment," he bluntly declared. "Your mother is welcome to see Adela at any time, but keep your father well off limits. That brother of yours, and your other sisters will probably visit you, and you them, but I'd appreciate your not telling them about our plans for Adela. We would have every clan elder in the country condemning us if word got out.

"Besides, the less Adela is seen in your home district, the better. The time will come when we have to provide a — shall we call it a new, suitable biography for your sister? Maybe a change of surname.

We'll never be able to do that if there is a whole semi-rural community in a position to contradict us."

Ujeni was not clear about what he meant. However, she had complete faith in his judgement, and she flew to his defence whenever Sam accused him of dominating their lives.

Keti stood smiling with false brightness. She also had her doubts about the Beauty Queen venture; how it was turning her friend into a vain, selfish individual, and how the man Joe Banda's word was law where Adela and Ujeni were concerned. She noticed that Sam was not there to say farewell to his wife, and wondered if his absence indicated a split in the family.

Just then, Adela impulsively hugged her. "Oh, I'm so glad you're here, Keti! I only wish that you were coming with us!"

Keti laughed, "Maybe some other time. You know that I'm working flat out for the exam, when I'm not at the hospice. But I'll be praying for you."

The final call for passengers for Nairobi to go through Customs and Immigration came over the airport Tannoy system, and Ujeni and Joe Banda, with scarcely a glance at Keti, hustled Adela out of sight.

Keti saw the tears in Adela's mother's eyes, and pressed the older woman's arm comfortingly as the two of them walked slowly and thoughtfully to where a taxi, paid for by Joe Banda, waited to take them home.

The four hour flight to Nairobi was uneventful, but as soon as Adela's party disembarked at Jomo Kenyatta International Airport she was immediately surrounded by a crowd of Press photographers waiting to take pictures of all the Pan Africa Oil beauty competitors as they arrived. Maxi had warned her to expect this sort of attention, and instructed her how to respond, but Adela still found it a nerve-racking experience. She was limp and perspiring by the time someone ushered her into an air-conditioned limousine and she was on her way to the Inter- Continental Hotel.

The novelty of being in a strange city, so much more modern than anything she was used to, soon revived her. She marvelled aloud at the amount of traffic on the roads and the vast skyscrapers piercing the landscape. The hotel, too, bedazzled her. She had never before been in such luxurious surroundings, and she was completely speechless at the sight of the enormous bouquet of roses, the champagne on ice, the basket of fruit, and the large box of Swiss chocolates, compliments of the competition's organisers, awaiting her in her room.

"I'll take these," Ujeni decided, gathering up the champagne and chocolates, and flouncing towards the door. "You know how too much sugar brings you out in spots. And go easy on that fruit. An upset stomach is the last thing we want to have to deal with!"

Adela pulled a face behind Ujeni's back and set about unpacking Lulu the doll, resplendent in a national costume identical to Adela's own, was placed in an easy chair facing the bed, so that she would be the last thing Adela saw before she slept, and the first thing when she awoke in the morning. There was little time to arrange her other personal belongings because all the contestants were to meet in the hotel ballroom for a briefing before dinner, and Ujeni and Maxi intended to spend the intervening hours in ensuring that Adela's appearance was impeccable.

Maxi had already commandeered one of the hotel staff to iron all Adela's clothes, and arranged for Nairobi's top hairdresser to be in attendance daily. Delicately applying shadow and liner to Adela's eyelids, while Ujeni carefully examined the girl's finger — and toe nails to see if any lacquer needed replacing, Maxi reminded her to keep aloof from the other contestants. "Take my word for it," she said. "They'll pretend that they are eager to be bosom pals with you, but they'll stab you in the back at the first opportunity! As far as they are concerned, you are serious competition, and none of them will like it."

"When can we go to the game park?" Adela asked.

The game park was one of the treats she had been promised, and she was bored by having to listen to nothing except talk of the contest.

"The organisers are taking all the contestants to the Nairobi National Park tomorrow afternoon," Yoweri, who had arrived with a sheaf of official-looking papers, including the itinerary, informed her. "There will to be a civic lunch with the Mayor of Nairobi on the day of the contest."

"That's bad planning," Maxi grumbled. "Adela had better cut that lunch. We're not risking a bloated stomach in the evening; and besides, we'll need every minute of the day to get her ready for the show."

"Right," Yoweri said as he made a note on the itinerary. "I'll let the organisers know that she is engaged elsewhere." His glance fell on the travelling clock standing on Adela's bedside table. "You ladies had better get a move on. The briefing begins in ten minutes."

Going down in the lift to the ballroom, they were joined by two more competitors, each with her chaperon. One was a sleek, coffee-coloured glamour girl. The other, an ebony beauty with long lustrous hair. Both girls smiled at Adela, but as she started to return their smiles, Maxi dug a warning elbow into her ribs, and Adela's face froze in a blank expression. The briefing lasted just over one hour, during which champagne was served, and Maxi, determinedly replacing Ujeni as chaperon for the occasion, pointedly requested pure orange juice for Adela. Adela viewed her rivals for the beauty crown with open interest — until Maxi sharply told her not to stare.

There were twenty contestants, and they represented various parts of Africa, although the contest was not run on the basis of nationally-chosen beauty queens. In Adela's eyes they were all in their different ways magnificent. Suddenly she did not feel as confident as Joe, Ujeni and Maxi had encouraged her to feel about walking away with the prize.

An entertaining young Kenyan who told everybody to call him Jack, broke in on her growing lack of confidence by explaining the itinerary and describing at length how the contest itself would proceed.

"I know it's all there in the information folders you have been given," he said, "but I'm a great believer in the personal touch. While you're here — under our wing, as it were — I hope that everyone of you will treat me as your best friend and father-confessor. It's my job to answer any questions you may have, as well as deal with any complaints."

Some of the contestants murmured appreciatively, so Jack went on to repeat what was already printed in the information package concerning the competition proceedings: namely, that the girls would first parade in their national costumes, then in identical gowns especially designed for Pan Africa Oil by a world-famous dress designer, and finally in evening gowns of their own choice. Stage rehearsals were to be held every morning at eleven o'clock, with a full dress rehearsal on the evening before the contest.

Some of the girls were anxious to know who the judges would be. Jack, however, refused to reveal their names, saying that they were to constitute an exciting surprise to the contestants, the general public and the Press.

"The judges names are being kept secret so that none of the contestants or their hangers-on can get to them in the hope of doing a deal," Maxi whispered to Adela. "You can bet your life that some of these girls are prepared to do anything — and I mean anything — to try influencing the judges in their favour!"

Adela was shocked. She looked around her and refused to believe maxi's wicked slander. Anyone could see that these girls had too much pride and self-respect to even consider doing anything so shameful. The more she looked at them, the more Adela was convinced that she might as well have stayed home.

She wished with all her heart that Keti was around to listen to her fears and doubts. In the circumstances, the only person to whom she dared voice them was Yoweri Wamala. In the two years that he had become part of the team grooming her for beauty stardom, Adela had overcome her initial resentment of him for the part he played in her having to leave St Mary's High School. For one thing, Yoweri's life, too, or so it seemed to Adela, was controlled by Joe Banda, and Ujeni

57

and Maxi treated him like a lowly messenger. Whether she liked it or not, Adela had come around to thinking that she and Yoweri Wamala had plenty in common.

As soon as she confided her misgivings, Yoweri made a hopeless gesture with his hands. "You mustn't lose confidence at this stage," he protested. "Tomorrow, the bookies will announce the odds on all of you girls taking part in the competition, and we're expecting the shortest odds to be on you!"

Adela could not understand what he was talking about, so he explained that bookies were people who ran gambling shops, who took bets from the general public on who or what would win in a variety of specific events. "Say I want to bet on your winning," he said, "and the odds on you are 10 – 1. Well, if I place a bet of one shilling on you, and you win, the bookies will pay me ten shillings. If you lose, I lose my one shilling bet."

Adela frowned. "It doesn't make sense. Where do these bookies get the money to pay you ten shillings for one shilling?"

Yoweri laughed. "Oh, they know what they are doing! There are always more losers than winners in their business. Which is why they shorten the odds on favourites, whether it's a race horse or a beauty queen! When it's pretty obvious who a winner will be, the bookies' odds can go as low 2 – 1. If what they call an 'outsider', meaning something or somebody who seems not to stand a chance, wins, and the odds stand at around 100 – 1, the bookies can find themselves out of pocket."

Adela thought about what he had said as soon as she was alone in her room, staring at herself in the large dressing-table mirror. It made her uncomfortable to know that to many people she was now in the same impersonal category as a racehorse; that their sole interest in her and the other contestants was their potential for the winning or losing of bets.

Later, at dinner, ignoring Maxi's repeated urging to smile and remember that she was on public display, Adela stared back impassively at the admiring men dining at nearby tables. 'I wonder how much they are prepared to bet on me?' was her cynical thought. 'Well, it serves them right if they lose a small fortune!'

Chapter 8

Three days before the Pan African Oil beauty competition, since publicity for the event was in full swing, the contestants were allowed very little time to themselves. With photographers constantly in attendance, none of them dared relax from the role of potential beauty queen, and the strain began to show on some of the less experienced. A girl from western Tanzania, for instance, suffered a crying fit when they were about to visit the Parliament building; and one from Burundi fainted on the steps of the Kenya National Theatre. Both had the satisfaction of seeing themselves pictured on the front pages of local newspapers, even if they were not posing glamorously.

Adela went along with the planned programme, but she was more and more puzzled by the attitude of Joe Banda, Maxi and Ujeni. Far from pressing her to do her best to outshine the other competitors, as they had upon their arrival in Nairobi, it seemed to Adela that they were actively engaged in making her look as inconspicuous as possible. Although her hair was professionally treated everyday, and her daily skin-care routine religiously followed, along with her manicure and pedicure, facial cosmetics were virtually abandoned.

Furthermore, she got the impression that Maxi deliberately kept back the more striking outfits in her wardrobe, and insisted that she wear only the plainest clothes.

Consequent upon this strange turn-about, the Press photographers soon lost interest in her, and instead aimed their cameras at the other girls taking part in the competition. Why, even at the full dress rehearsal, from which members of the Press were excluded, Adela had been appalled at having to appear in clothes which, apart from the Pan Africa Oil specially-designed gown to be worn at one stage by all the contestants, she knew had never been intended for more than ordinary, everyday wear.

She wondered what had happened to the beautiful things for which she had spent hours being measured and fitted, and she worried about what she could have done wrong to bring about such a drastic change of heart in Joe Banda, Maxi and Ujeni.

"No need to worry," Yoweri cheerfully assured her, after she tentatively asked him what was the matter. "It's all part of Joe's strategy. On our first day here, we were what is called 'testing the water.' In other words, you were made to look your best, and you were the bookies favourite to win the contest the moment your picture appeared in the papers, so the odds on you were very low. As soon as we knew the score, it was Joe's idea to tone you down so that the Press concentrated on some of the other contestants and you slipped into the background. He knows what he's doing, our man!" Yoweri exclaimed, as he shook his head and grinned admiringly. "In two days the odds on your winning have slipped from 5 – 1 to 20 – 1 that's what the bookies think your chances are!"

"What is this bookies business, and what has it got to do with Joe Banda?" Adela asked angrily.

Yoweri's eyes widened. "Don't tell me you didn't know? Joe is waiting until the odds against you soar even higher, then he's placing a bet on you to win five thousand US dollars!"

"What if I don't win?" Adela sulkily demanded.

"You will," Yoweri grimly nodded. "Or shall we say, you had better, if you know what's good for you!"

Adela now understood why Maxi had earlier that day ruined the effect of one of her more reasonably attractive dresses by making her wear with it a totally inappropriate head-tie and strings of cheap beads. It made her bitter to realise that to Joe Banda she was nothing more than a means for him to make large amounts of money. All his talk of a lucrative career for her was, Adela convinced herself, rubbish, and his occasional 'kind uncle' act, a joke. Had she not been secretly frightened by Yoweri's grim advice that she had better win — and he had made it sound as if the consequences of losing did not bear thinking about — Adela would have thrown caution to the wind and somehow made her way home. As things stood, she knew that she was a helpless pawn in the hands of unscrupulous people, and they included her own sister. Again, she found herself yearning for the presence of her friend Keti, as well as her brother-in-law, Sam, the only two people in whom she had complete trust that their affection and concern for her was genuine.

On the day of the competition, Maxi and Ujeni were knocking at her bedroom door to awaken Adela from a troubled sleep at six in the morning.

"Come on, girl!" Ujeni chided. "The manager has arranged for us to use the gym before the official opening time. Get into your leotard. You can have an hour's work-out before breakfast."

Adela groaned and yawned.

"Do as Ujeni tells you," Maxi admonished. "This will probably be the most important day of your life, so let's start as we mean to go on."

After the strenuous work-out to disco music, Adela was allowed a shower and later breakfasted on orange juice, pawpaw, dry toast and coffee. Then a young woman arrived in her room to give her a full body massage and afterwards apply a special herbal face pack. More time was spent on a manicure and a pedicure. Adela tried to rest, as instructed by Maxi and Ujeni, for a couple of hours before the hairdresser was expected, but she was hungry. The meagre lunch of hard-boiled eggs, lettuce and tomato, had left her longing for a steaming plateful of plantain and groundnut sauce with dried fish. She felt resentful at Ujeni for removing the huge box of Swiss chocolates, and in a rebellious mood, she rang room service and asked for a dish of grilled lake fish and spinach to be brought to her room.

She was half-way through eating the fish, and enjoying every mouthful, when the door was flung open and Maxi, Ujeni and Joe Banda stormed in.

"What do you think you are doing? Luck for us that Yoweri spotted a waiter bringing a tray in here!" Ujeni angrily snatched the plate of fish away. "Are you mad — or are you deliberately trying to ruin our plans — the hard work we have put into you over the past two years?"

he was half-way through eating the fish... [when] Ujeni angrily snatched the late of fish away

"I was hungry," Adela said, bursting into tears.

"Oh, God! For Heaven's sake don't cry!" Maxi exclaimed. "This is one day when you can't afford red puffy eyes!"

She rifled the room's hospitality fridge for ice, and, having found a trayful, rushed to the bathroom to dislodge the cubes and wrap them in a facecloth. "Here — apply this to your eyes. And if you must weep, do us all a favour and keep your tears till after you've won!"

Joe Banda, who at first appeared to be in a tearing temper, now smiled comfortingly at Adela and patted her shoulder. "She's having an attack of nerves, and it's only natural in the circumstances," he said. And to Ujeni, "Let her have the fish. We don't want her walking on stage with a rumbling tummy, do we?"

"Nor a bloated one . . ." Maxi began until Joe motioned her to silence.

Despite being grateful for his surprising understanding, Adela discovered that her appetite had gone. Listlessly, she accepted the continuation of the beautifying of herself from top to toe, and closed her ears to the hairdresser's endless chatter as he arranged her hair in a deceptively simple face-flattering style.

The national costume intended to be worn for the competition, and so far kept out of sight, was at last produced. It was a marvellous creation of the finest silk in soft iridescent colours. As Adela stepped into it, she caught sight of herself in a full-length mirror, and gasped. So used had she become over the preceding couple of days to seeing a thoughtlessly-dressed drab, that the reflected image of a gloriously perfect creature in a gown of utter splendour made her catch her breath.

"Yes," Maxi smugly remarked. "In my humble opinion, those other girls might as well pack up now and go home. We have a definite winner here!"

Suddenly, Adela, regardless of Maxi's confidence in her, was overwhelmed by stage fright. A physical sickness enveloped her and she trembled in every limb. She knew beyond any doubt that she would never be able to take to the stage with the graceful ease she had long been taught to master. The thought of being stared at by an audience made up mostly of important people made her panic. She cried out that she couldn't go through with it.

"Oh, yes you can," the ever resourceful Maxi dug into her handbag and produced a bottle of tiny white pills. "Here, take two of these with a glass of water. I guarantee that you'll soon feel on top of the world and ready to tackle anything." She emptied two of the pills into the palm of Adela's hand, and two more into her own. "See," she remarked, "you're not the only one who is nervous. I have not the slightest doubt about your winning, but all the excitement is beginning to get to me!"

Thirty minutes after the pills were swallowed, Adela was escorted to where the other contestants waited, back-stage. She alone was ready for the first parading in national costume: most of the others were still touching-up their make-up and making last minute adjustments to their clothes in a large communal dressing-room with bright light bulbs surrounding a row of mirrors above a long, shared dressing-table.

Jack came forward to meet Adela and her retinue comprising Joe Banda, Ujeni, Maxi, and tagging along behind them, Yoweri Wamala.

"I'm sorry," he smilingly apologised, "only the contestants are allowed back here. Chaperons and others are out front. Special tables have been reserved for you."

Maxi looked appealingly at him. "Couldn't you possibly make an exception in our case? Adela is not used to being on her own, and this is her first contest."

Jack shook his head. "Sorry, madam. Rules are rules. I can see that Adela is ready for the national costume parade, but for the Pan Africa Oil dress section, as well as the evening gown for the finale, she'll have to be like the others and use this dressing-room. I believe that everything was made clear on this subject in the information sheets you were given."

As he spoke, he stared curiously at Adela. Then he added, "I take it that this really is Adela? I mean she looks totally different from the girl at yesterday's dress rehearsal — and I swear that I don't remember ever seeing this . . . this fantastic outfit!"

Maxi fluttered her hands in pretended helplessness. "Oh, yes, this is Adela, all right. and I know the girls are supposed to parade in the clothes they wore at the dress rehearsal. Unfortunately, a terrible thing happened! My fault, I'm afraid — I was clumsy with a hot iron, so we had to dress Adela in the only other national costume she's brought with her!"

Jack, still staring, said "Well, in that case, I'm sure we can bend the rules. But please bring the other two gowns she requires to this dressing-room for her to dress herself. I'm afraid I can't make an exception of her beyond allowing her to wear this replacement outfit."

Normally, Adela would have been frantic at the thought of having to cope alone. For two years, either Maxi or Ujeni, and sometimes both, had attended to her hair, her make-up and her clothes. She couldn't remember when she had last slipped into as little as a pair of jeans without the help of either one of them. She mildly wondered how she would manage. But the pills Maxi had given her were doing wonders for Adela's ego. She experienced no pangs of uncertainty as she waved the reluctant party off to join the audience, and a superior smile hovered around her lips as she took in the nineteen glamour girls comprising her rivals for the Pan Africa Oil beauty crown. No longer did she see them as superior to herself. Some of them were absolutely pathetic, she loftily decided. A soft giggle escaped her lips. She knew that she would win.

Chapter 9

A strident fanfare of trumpets announced the start of the Pan Africa Oil beauty contest, and Jack marshalled the girls into line according to the number they were given to wear on a ribbon attached to one wrist. Adela took it as a good sign that she was allocated number seven, the same number she had been given in her first and hitherto only beauty competition. To the strains of a popular dance tune, the twenty, well-rehearsed girls first took to the stage in a simple dance consisting mainly of twirling and posing, but which was nevertheless picturesque and well-appreciated by the audience. Then, as Jack announced their names and countries of origin, they paraded individually and received separate rounds of applause.

Adela smiled a secret amused smile as she noted that nearly all the other contestants were blatantly swinging their hips and throwing inviting glances at the two male judges on the panel. When her turn came, she did exactly as Maxi had taught her. She walked and turned with elegant dignity, like a queen, and bestowed on the panel of judges a shyly polite yet impersonal glance.

The significance of the thundering applause and cheers failed to make any impression upon Adela, however, for her heart had turned a somersault as she recognised one of the judges as Byron Warlock, the Oscar-winning Black American movie star. The screen did not do him justice: it failed to capture in full the overpowering magnetism of his glowing vitality apparent in the crispness of his hair, the clear brightness of his eyes, and his muscular body, a legacy of his earlier days as a gold medallist athlete. Adela and her classmates had adored him. To them, Byron Warlock was perfection; he also indirectly helped them conform to Sr. Felicia's strict teachings on maidenly purity, since their schoolgirl hearts beat for him alone and they tended to regard other males of their acquaintance as practically sub-human. Adela, seeing her hero in the flesh, was momentarily thrown off balance, but after one swift astonished glance, she avoided looking directly at him, and fixed her mind on making a graceful exit.

Back in the communal dressing-room, she found Maxi waiting for her with the gown designed to promote the Pan African Oil logo. Since Jack was kept on-stage in his role of master of ceremonies, and could be heard introducing the pop trio who were to entertain the guests while the contestants prepared for the second part of the competition, she was able, without interference, to help Adela change outfits and carry away the national costume.

"And never mind what that man says," she hissed at her. "I'll deliver your evening gown when it's time for you to wear it, and not before. From the way that crowd out there went crazy over you, you're already the winner. But we're not taking risks. These jealous cows . . . " she threw a contemptuous glance at the other competitors, "are not above damaging your clothes in the hope of ruining your chances!"

Adela was frankly amused by Maxi's suspicions of the other contestants, and was sure they were groundless, until she witnessed one of them deliberately smudge with tinted foundation cream an elaborate dress hanging on a rack in one of the open cupboards, and which belonged to the ebony beauty whom Adela had met in the hotel lift. This girl, unknown to Adela, was, at the last shouting of odds, the bookies' current favourite to win. Apparently, Joe Banda's crafty move to make Adela look like a poor relation had succeeded beyond his wildest dreams. Nevertheless, the ebony beauty had also received tremendous applause from the audience, many of whom had placed 5-1 bets on her winning.

The forty-five minutes of cabaret entertainment between each section of the competition gave the judges time to compare and collate the marks they had individually awarded to the contestants, bringing about the elimination of six girls who received the lowest totals.

Adela had not really understood Jack's explanation of how various contestants would not make it past the first national costume parade, and that others would lose out in the second heat. He had tried to soften the blow by pointing out that those eliminated could still take part in all the events marking the end of the competition, and by asserting that whatever the outcome, he was sure he could count on every one of them to be good sports.

When the first eliminations were announced, however, there was no sign of the good sportsmanship on which Jack had depended. Girls who five minutes earlier had been purring and preening, turned savage as they heard of their elimination from the contest amplified to the audience and the dressing-room. They accused the organisers of rigging the contest, and made wild threats of revenge. One girl in particular and Adela was secretly satisfied to note that it was the same girl responsible for disfiguring the ebony beauty's gown, first wept, then accused Adela and the ebony beauty of sleeping with Jack in order to stay in the contest.

"Not together, I hope!" the ebony beauty chuckled, winking at Adela.

Adela herself was badly shaken. For the past two years she had been protected from any so-called 'dirty talk', and to be accused by a complete stranger of having an immoral relationship with a casual acquaintance upset her more than she showed. Maxi, taking further advantage of Jack's absence from the dressing-room, miraculously appeared at that moment. She knew Adela well enough to detect signs of distress.

"I'm just checking that outfit doesn't need a pin anywhere," she explained, tugging the garment into place. "No. I think it's all right as long as you don't droop!" Then, quietly, "What's wrong, child?"

Adela told her, fighting back tears.

Maxi, without a word, produced the bottle of tiny white pills and handed one to Adela. Adela gratefully accepted it, and by the time the interval was over, she was once again beginning to feel pleasantly confident.

Wearing the gown specially-designed for the Pan Africa Oil Beauty Queen competitors, Adela stepped on-stage for a second time, and again retained the remote regal composure instilled into her by Maxi. She paid absolutely no attention to the wildest applause so far of the

Maxı... produced the bottle of tıny white pılls and handed one to Adela

evening, nor to the standing ovation led by Chief Atalifu, Chairman of Pan African Oil. She was nevertheless conscious throughout of Byron Warlock's eyes upon her and was surprised to detect a look of concern. But once again Adela deliberately refrained from allowing her gaze to linger on him. Hadn't Maxi impressed upon her that 'ogling', as Maxi termed it, any of the judges was third-rate and cheapening, as well as bound to go down badly with the other members of the panel? She made one small deviation from Maxi's strict teaching, though, and it was the result of a natural reaction: when someone in the audience threw a bunch of roses that scattered as it hit the stage, Adela picked up one of the flowers, kissed its scented petals, and made three graceful curtsies addressed to everybody in the packed ballroom, before making another dignified exit. Understandably, the audience went wild.

Maxi hurried into the dressing-room with Adela's evening dress within seconds of Jack announcing the contestants who were to remain in the competition for the final section and those who were eliminated. She was in a fever of excitement. Hugging Adela, she cried, "You clever girl! We're all so proud of you! You were absolutely splendid! Now, let's get you into this — and keep well away from the other girls. They know you've won, and it wouldn't surprise me if they tried to rip it off your back!"

She held out the gown that had been hidden from prying eyes like a state secret. But she re-covered it protectively as soon as she saw the behaviour of some of the second batch of eliminated contestants. They glared with naked hatred and jealousy at Adela.

"Maybe we had better wait a while," Maxi murmured. "You sit on this stool by the door — don't hesitate to make a run for it if a fight breaks out. I'll be back with this dress just before you are due on stage."

Adela was reluctant to see her go. The dressing-room was suddenly rowdy. The ebony beauty had discovered the damage to her evening gown, and was in tears; while two of the eliminated girls loudly joined their predecessors in making accusations of the contest being rigged, and that the girls fortunate enough to still be competing were there only because they had the morals of alley-cats.

Somebody came with refreshments on a tray. Adela nibbled a cheese sandwich and drank a soda. She was not really hungry, but eating and drinking gave her something to do. She watched impassively as a woman from the hotel laundry arrived to try and remove the stain from the ebony beauty's gown, and her mind roamed over what would be the reaction of the rich, well-fed guests if they knew the sordidness of life backstage for these girls with naked ambitions to be beauty queens.

Adela had been mildly astonished to learn from scraps of conversation heard in the dressing-room that none of the other contestants had had anything like the two years' pampered grooming that she herself had undergone at the hands of Maxi, Ujeni and Joe Banda. They were aiming to reach the top of the beauty queen tree by their own efforts, and from some of the things some said, it seemed that quite a few of them regarded their near-perfect bodies as assets to be used indiscriminately in the climb towards their goal. The Miss World competition was their goal, and they were prepared to do anything to get there.

Apart from a timid smile from the ebony beauty, who Adela now knew as Josephine from the Ivory Coast, the other six girls competing in the final section of the Pan Africa Oil contest studiously ignored her. So she sat in uncomfortable isolation while everybody, including those already eliminated, perfected hair and make-up, and carefully drew on the elaborate dresses intended for the final heat of the contest and the grand finale of the evening in which all twenty contestants were scheduled to parade on stage.

Maxi arrived breathlessly with Adela's evening gown and slippers as Jack could be heard from the stage introducing the last cabaret act. Contrasting sharply with most of those chosen by the other competitors in vividly elaborate fabrics, Adela's gown, copied down to the last detail from a model pictured in *Vogue* fashion magazine, was a clever arrangement of Grecian drapes in the purest white chiffon, covering her from neck to toe, yet leaving her arms bare and emphasising the virginal curve of her breasts and the slenderness of her waist.

After applying a light coating of face powder to Adela's nose and twitching a wayward lock of hair back into place, Maxi stood back and regarded with delight her work of two years. "It was worth every moment!" she declared in a choking voice and smiling through tears.

"Joe is right. You really are something special. Now walk out there and win that Pan Africa Oil crown!"

The eight remaining contestants together paraded the stage to a romantic ballad sung by one of East Africa's most famous entertainers, while again Jack listed their names and countries of origin for the benefit of the audience. Then they were called upon one by one to answer questions from the judges and be awarded marks for personality and deportment.

Although well-schooled in this aspect of beauty competitions by Maxi and Joe Banda, Adela had always dreaded the moment when she would be expected to speak into a microphone. It was bad enough knowing that she might have to answer the judges' questions with lies, as her replies had to be in accordance with the new biography prepared for her by Joe; it was worse having whatever she said relayed aloud to an audience of hundreds. But Maxi's mystery pills worked wonders for her self confidence. She even managed, stepping towards the judges' table and accepting the hand-mike, to acknowledge with a shy, dimpling smile the 'Oohs!' and 'Aahs!" provoked by the full view of her gown, as well as the admiring catcalls and whistles from some of the cruder members of the audience.

"Tell us, my dear, what induced you to enter the Pan Africa Oil beauty competition?" the first judge, the head of a beauty products corporation, asked her.

Adela smiled modestly at him, and repeated what Joe Banda had told her to say, dropping her voice to a low huskiness as taught by Maxi. "This is my first beauty contest, sir. I entered because some of my friends dared me to. And I'm finding it great fun! Everyone has been so kind."

The judge raised his eyebrows, and Adela modestly hung her head in the well-rehearsed way that was reminiscent of a fragile flower drooping on a delicate stem.

"So you are not what we in the business term a career beauty queen?"

"Oh, no!" Adela protested, blinking to indicate that the mere idea shocked her. "I'm a student, and I hope to enter university after my next exams."

The judge seemed impressed. He said, "What a refreshing change from beauty contestants who only want to travel and meet people . . ."

"What do you hope to study at university?" Byron Warlock put in, grinning in a mocking manner that Adela found disturbing. She could not avoid facing him, and she prayed that he was not aware of the increase in her pulse rate as she tried to answer him gravely.

"If I'm successful in the exam, I want to do Sociology," she lied. Joe had decided on Sociology for an answer to an expected question because he believed it would show Adela as a caring, community-minded individual.

"And what do you hope to do when you get a degree?" Byron relentlessly asked her.

"I shall work where I am most needed in our community, of course," Adela parroted the phrase instilled into her by Joe with an air of producing an original flow of words, and was annoyed that her questioner seemed not in the least impressed by her answer.

The third judge, a glamorous woman journalist famous for her acid criticism of United Nations agencies as well as her support for human rights groups, wanted to know Adela's views on the work being done to safeguard teenage schoolgirls from unwanted pregnancies.

Magical pills or no magical pills, Adela was momentarily at a loss for an answer. She stared blankly at the woman, and flinched as the journalist cynically continued. "Oh, come on! If you're so keen to be a sociologist, don't tell me that you have not yet interested yourself in this extremely serious problem?"

"I . . . I have't had time to study it," Adela mumbled.

Then she remembered overhearing Ujeni's bitter comments on how a boy responsible for impregnating the daughter of a friend was allowed back in school while the girl was immediately expelled. Quoting her sister almost verbatim, Adela said in a stronger voice,

"One way of safeguarding schoolgirls would be to make sure that boys responsible for getting girls pregnant receive the same punishment and are not allowed to continue in school. And whether it's a schoolboy or a sugar daddy who is responsible for a pregnancy, they ought under the law be made to financially support the mother and child. I think that this is one area in which the social services in my own country, and very likely in many others, are ineffectual."

Amid cheering from women in the audience, the woman journalist gave Adela an encouraging smile. "Well said! It's plain to everybody that this is one beauty who is rather more than a pretty face!"

Afterwards, Adela vaguely remembered leaving the stage to tumultuous applause and under a positive bombardment of flowers. This time, she did not select a flower and kiss it. Instead, she, paused centre stage, arms outstretched as though to embrace all those who hysterically shrieked that the Pan Africa Oil beauty crown should be hers, then bowed in acknowledgement and walked quietly into the wings.

There was a brief interlude before Jack announced the winner together with the first and second runners-up, and this time the girls did not return to the dressing-room. They stood out of sight of the audience, tense and silent, and hopeful concerning their own prospects to the very last minute.

The coffee-coloured glamour girl was listed third and Josephine from Ivory Coast second. "And now, Ladies and Gentlemen," Jack shouted into the microphone, "the moment we've all been waiting for:

the judges are unanimous in choosing Adela from that beautiful land-locked country, Matola, Miss Pan Africa Oil!"

His words from the naming of Adela onwards, were lost in a storm of cheers, clapping and loud hoots of joy.

An immense blue velvet cloak that swept the floor for metres behind her, was draped around her shoulders, complementing the classic lines of the white chiffon gown, and as she was seated on a magnificent white raised throne of impressive proportions, the Chairman of Pan Africa Oil mounted the three broad steps and personally placed upon her head a dazzling crown of brilliant semi-precious stones.

She was at long last a real beauty queen.

Chapter 10

Adela willingly gave herself up to the bevy of flashing cameras, the endless congratulations, the masses of floral tributes, the smiles and kisses from her former rivals who only a short time ago had clearly wished her dead. She revelled in the flattering fuss and attention. She experienced no pangs of guilt when Joe Banda gave reporters copies of her biography which described her as the only daughter of a roving diplomat from a family with aristocratic connections, gave her age as 18, claimed fictional academic successes, and stated that she was a serious student whose sole ambition was to work for society's underprivileged.

She was not to know that a different kind of pill pressed upon her by Maxi who had wrongly imagined that Adela was cracking up under the strain of so much excitement, its effects heightened by the combination of those she had earlier taken, was responsible for the surge of reckless abandonment. The usually reserved, self-aware Adela was taken over completely by an outgoing, devil-may-care creature who was convinced that she could conquer the world, and who experienced sickly-sweet sentiments towards everybody and everything in sight.

She managed with difficulty to subdue her wild exuberance and retain an air of modest dignity when Chief Atalifu offered his arm, and the two of them headed a procession comprising the beauty contestants, the judges, local dignitaries and other invited guests to his penthouse suite adjoining a wide terrace overlooking the city, where a sumptuous buffet supper awaited them.

But she found it hard to suppress a giggle when it transpired that Maxi, Joe Banda, Ujeni and Yoweri were excluded from this favoured gathering. Their furious protests went unheeded by the competition's organisers, and so Adela was able to enjoy her triumph alone and to the full. As the guest of honour, she was saved from having to join the crowd and making a bee-line for the buffet. The Chairman himself served her with prawn cocktail, a breast of chicken on a bed of rice and mushrooms accompanied by delicate asparagus tips, and finally a bowl of wild strawberries and cream. Adela ate heartily and drank glass after glass of champagne which she was beginning to find very much to her taste.

After the meal, she listened dreamily to several speeches by local notables, all of them in praise of Pan Africa Oil's contribution to the Kenyan economy. Adela remained contentedly sipping champagne on a comfortable sofa when formality was dropped and the party livened up considerably. Carpets were rolled back, and guests took to the floor to dance in a variety of styles.

As Adela was fascinatingly watching one of her former rivals coaxing a perspiring stout gentleman into strenuous exertion on the dance floor, a quiet voice in her ear said, "What are you on, kid?"

Startled, she raised her head and found Byron Warlock standing over her.

"I'm sorry?" she said, breathless at having him so close.

He gave her a small, tight smile. "I think you heard me. I asked what you're on."

The question made no sense to Adela. "I'm sorry," she apologetically repeated. "I don't understand you."

Byron sat down beside her and heaved a theatrical sigh before saying "Listen! You can come clean with me. What sort of dope are you on, that's what I want to know. And don't deny that you're taking something — I could tell from your eyes before you approached the judges' table this evening. And now you've been sitting here for a couple of hours with that spaced-out look on your face. I'm surprised that nobody else has noticed it!"

"I don't take drugs, if that's what you mean!" she protested. "What right have you to suggest such a thing? Joe and Maxi would never allow it — and my sister Ujeni would kill them if they did!"

"Who are Joe and Maxi?" he asked, and Adela, her tongue loosened by the amount of champagne she had taken, coming on top of Maxi's pills, happily related with a sentimental gratitude quite different from her usual hidden resentment, of the three who ruled her life, and the part they played in bringing about her victory.

Byron listened to her mindless chatter with an expression of growing contempt. Finally he commented, "Flesh merchants! That's what we call them in the States. They take a kid like you and turn her into a beautiful walking, talking, living doll. Then when they've made as much as they can out of her, and she's past it, they throw her on the scrap-heap and she's lucky if she doesn't end up a junkie!"

Adela was too busy admiring his incredibly good looks to take in what he said. Never in her wildest dreams could she have imagined his sitting near her and talking to her, as she believed, like an old friend. The meaningless smile on her face broadened at the thought, and noticing it, Byron snapped "Ok, I believe you when you say you're not a regular — but how about this evening, don't deny that you accepted a little something to — how shall I put it? Calm you down or pep you up?"

She nodded her head childishly. "That's right. Maxi gave me a pill after I cried , then another, then another . . . Maxi is very good to me. I love Maxi. I love . . ." her head slumped on her chest, and Byron quickly jumped up to stand in front of her to shield her from the other guests.

"And I bet your beloved Maxi forgot to tell you that booze and pills don't mix," he grimly muttered.

Having shaken Adela until she was briefly able to stand, he took her in his arms and danced her out of the room, thankful for the number of party gatecrashers who swelled the throng on the dance floor so that he had to squeeze his way through. From there he guided her to a lift and then along a corridor to her room, the number of which he knew because, as one of the judges of the beauty contest, he had felt obliged to arrange for flowers to reach her next morning.

At the door of room 109 he faced the problem of how to get in. Adela had not carried the key, and Byron discarded the idea of dumping her in the corridor while he collected her key from the reception desk. The situation was saved by the appearance of one of the hotel's assistant managers. Byron hailed him with relief. "Look, man, the excitement has been too much for Pan Africa Oil's beauty queen. The kid is worn-out, finished, kaput. Do me a favour and get the key to her room so that she can rest."

The assistant manager was overwhelmed at being alone in the combined company of a Hollywood star and the young woman who had so recently won acclaim as a sensational beauty. He stammered his willingness to help and fled to the reception, praying that nobody else would gain entry to the room before he obtained the key and rob him of his chance to mix with a couple of celebrities.

While waiting for his return, Byron propped the limp Adela against the door, and pretended to be holding an animated conversation with her on the few occasions that other hotel guests passed by. As most of the time Adele's eyes were closed, he was at liberty to examine the incredible perfection of her features and skin. Never had he seen such naturally long eyelashes, and he marvelled at the graceful sweep of her cheek and throat. His fans would have been surprised, or rather disturbed, had they witnessed the regret and despair that momentarily clouded his uniquely handsome face. It was a moment glimpsed only by the little assistant manager who arrived triumphantly with the key to room 109. Byron managed a wry smile. "Well, man, now you're here, you can help me put this young lady to bed!"

The assistant manager was speechless with the excitement of it all. What a tale he would have to tell everybody at home! This was exactly the situation of which he had often dreamed. Together, he and Byron arranged Adela on the bed, and they were about to leave when she suddenly moaned, "I am going to be sick!"

"Leave it to me!" Byron said to the assistant manager, unceremoniously dragging her off the bed and into the bathroom.

Byron. ... unceremoniously dragging her off the bed and into the bathroom

At the same time, another guest tapped on the door and anxiously called "I believe the assistant manager is there? Dirty water is shooting up through the plughole of my washbasin! Please can he come and attend to it?"

The assistant manager hastened to attend to the troubled guest and her washbasin, and Byron, pressing a hundred dollar bill into the man's hand, assured him that he could manage Adela on his own.

"When she's finished throwing-up, I'll leave her," he said. "I think she'll be all right."

"Perhaps some coffee?" the assistant manager eagerly suggested, but Byron considered lots of cold water the best remedy.

Adela emerged from the bathroom looking like a refugee from a disaster area. The model gown was ruined and she herself was a wreck. Gritting his teeth, Byron insisted that she take a shower and generally clean herself up.

"I will if you promise that you'll wait here," she declared, deliberately petulant.

"Okay. But move it, lady, will you?" he shrugged resignedly and sat down on a roomy sofa.

She was away for about fifteen minutes, and when she eventually tottered out of the bathroom she was wearing only a towel. "Get some clothes on," Byron gruffly told her, rising to his feet and averting his eyes from the enticingly shapely legs. "I'm out of here!"

"No you're not!" she swayed across to the room's hospitality fridge and removed a bottle of champagne. "Ujeni was here when this was delivered. Compliments of the hotel management, just before the competition, but she forgot to take it with her!" she giggled. "Come on, let's open it!"

"No. You've had enough. You had better go to bed," he said as he yawned and stretched. "That's where I'm heading. Goodnight, Miss Pan Africa Oil!"

82

"No!" Adela rushed at him and gripped him tightly around the waist. "No! You can't leave me — you're my best friend! I've loved you all my life!"

Byron realised with a shock that she was still under the influence of drugs and drink, and again wondered what on earth the woman Maxi had supplied her with.

"How about some coffee?" he asked, wishing he had taken up the assistant manager's earlier offer. "I'll call room service."

"No!" Adela's voice rose on an hysterical note.

"OK! OK!" He waved a conciliatory hand. The last thing he needed was a drunk-drugged teenager attracting attention by bellowing at him in a hotel bedroom.

"We'll have one drink then I'll go. I need my rest as much as you do."

The uncorked champagne sent a spurt of foaming bubbles to the ceiling, and Adela pranced excitedly around the room, heedless of the towel slipping to reveal her nakedness. Byron gulped his drink, anxious to escape. But suddenly she was winding herself around him and the towel lay in a heap on the floor.

"Stop that!" he exclaimed, fighting her off.

Her response was a more frantic clinging to him and a search for his mouth with her own, in between wild declarations of love. Attempting to free himself, he slapped her face — hard. The slap did not have the desired effect. If anything, it inspired Adela to greater effort in hanging on to him.

In the ensuing scuffle Byron found himself stumbling with her onto the bed. It was an uneven struggle. She held him in a vice-like grip which belied her fragile appearance, and despite his resolute good intentions, he was helpless against the attraction of that beautiful nubile young body.

Chapter 11

While the Chairrman of Pan Africa Oil was entertaining in his penthouse suite, another, less prestigious party was going on in one of the reception halls of the Inter-Continental Hotel. The chaperons, managers, and what-will-you of the beauty competition contestants were gathered together to drink, eat, dance and talk shop. Naturally, Adela's entourage were given pride of place, for after all, hadn't they produced the winner? The homage paid to them — even to such low life as Yoweri Wamala — in some part made up for their being excluded from the penthouse party, and they basked happily in Adela's reflected glory.

Joe Banda was easily reconciled to being bypassed by the Chairman of Pan Africa Oil because he looked forward to collecting his winnings from the betting shops. The odds against Adela's winning had not quite reached the 50-1 mark, as he had hoped, but at 45-1 he had no reason for complaint. Cunningly, he had spread his bets between four bookies, so as to arouse no suspicion of something fishy going on, and tomorrow he would collect his reward. Converted into US dollars at the current favourable rate of exchange, it promised to be a satisfying sum. Then, too, there was Adela's prize money of five thousand US dollars, plus all that she was likely to earn from the multi-media, multi-million dollar Pan Africa Oil promotion campaign. Yes, Joe Banda had picked a winner, all right, and he smiled as he thought of the fortune now within his grasp. As the chief shareholder in the company formed to promote Adela as a professional beauty queen, his would be the lion's share of everything she made.

Yoweri Wamala had started off by enjoying the party, finding it a pleasant change to be treated with respect. Yes, he was learning the intricacies of big business all the time from Joe Banda who paid him a substantial salary, and he, too, had made a comfortable amount of money by betting on Adela when she was rated a not even also-ran by the bookies. But nothing altered the fact that he was, to all intents and purposes, nothing more than a sort of messenger or what might be termed a favoured junior clerk to Joe, Maxi and Ujeni. He spent most of his time running errands for all three of them, and they seemed to forget that he had feelings just like everybody else. Yoweri's dignity suffered daily at their hands, and often, after a particularly humiliating incident, he dreamed up drastic forms of revenge.

He experienced another bout of extreme distress at the party, which ruined the whole event for him, when Ujeni imperiously ordered him to fetch her a drink, and Maxi curtly told him to shut up as he was in the middle of fondly describing to an interested group how Adela, now Miss Pan Africa Oil, was his personal discovery. Miserably, he left the party and took himself off to an all-night bar, there to drink and dwell on his misfortunes. The more he drank, the more he considered that he had made a mistake in accepting Joe Banda's offer of a responsible job.

In the old days, Yoweri nostalgically recalled, he had been his own master — and there were no haughty females to treat him like dirt beneath their feet. True, his former life precluded smart offices, luxury hotels and rubbing shoulders with the great and the good, not to mention the chance to travel. Before being taken up by Joe Banda, Yoweri had never been outside his own country or worn anything near the expensive suits which he now took for granted. All the same, Yoweri regretted his lack of independence. The trouble was that he had grown used to easy living and it made him bitter to reflect that he had outgrown his former life-style, that there was no going back.

Vengeance, however, for the slights he had suffered, played heavily on his mind. Somehow he would find a way of hitting back at the three people who consistently made him feel inferior. Such were his thoughts as he staggered back to his room on the same floor as Adela's.

He emerged from the lift in time to see Byron Warlock letting himself out of Adela's room. Even in his drunken state, Yoweri was slightly shocked to notice how haggard and, yes, frightened the superstar looked. He watched him half-run towards the lifts at the other end of the corridor, and puzzled over how the man had come to be in Adela's room. 'Was he a thief'? Yoweri wondered, for as far as he knew, Adela herself was supposed to be still in the penthouse at a party expected to go on till dawn.

"None of my business," he at last mumbled, moving towards his own room. "Everything the girl owns was paid for by Joe Banda, so if Hollywood's golden boy has helped himself to a few valuables, good luck to him. It will do Joe good to lose out for a change."

Then his mood altered. He had to admit that Adela had of late been very considerate of him. In fact it could even be said that she looked to him for comfort and was the only person in their group to seriously listen to anything he had to say. No, Yoweri, decided in a fit of drunken sentimentality that brought tears to his eyes, he wished no harm to that girl, and he would not like to see her upset because something she valued was stolen. With an aggression born of booze, he clenched his fists, lowered his head menacingly and, swaying on his feet, swore that he would kill anybody who dared to harm a hair of Adela's head.

Without thought or reason, he made for her room, brokenly muttering that she was his discovery and that it was time Joe Banda remembered that important fact. The effort brought him out in a alcoholic sweat, and to steady himself he leaned against the door, tumbling backwards as it swung open beneath his weight.

For a few moments Yoweri lay across the threshold, guiltily convinced that he had somehow broken the lock. Then he scrambled clumsily to his feet, his one idea being to leave the scene of what he imagined was his crime. A long drawn-out sigh coming from the direction of the bed stopped him in his tracks. The hair on the nape of his neck rose, and Yoweri stiffened. Slowly he turned, bracing himself for he knew not what, and gasped unbelievingly at the sight of Adela lying naked in the midst of a crumpled bedcover and pillows. As a moaned "Byron!" escaped her lips, and she stirred voluptuously, Yoweri bolted.

As soon as he reached the safety of his own room, his brain cleared sufficiently for him to realise the significance of what he had witnessed. He knew that the matter ought to be reported to Joe, and yet he hesitated. Yes, Joe Banda provided his bread with a good helping of butter, and was entitled to Yoweri's loyalty. On the other hand, he could not face destroying Adela's growing trust by telling tales about her. Mixed with these feelings was an almost cynical delight that after two years of Joe and his female partners keeping the girl like a nun in a luxury convent, in that every minute of her day was supervised or chaperoned, and the company she was allowed to keep carefully vetted, Adela had slipped through the protective net on her first appearance as a beauty queen. In the end, Yoweri decided that it was in his best interest to do nothing. After all, he was not paid to be a personal bodyguard, and trouble, his own or that of anybody else, was the last thing he wanted. He took a hefty swig of neat whisky, then fell heavily into bed.

* * *

The next morning Adela could hardly raise her head from the pillow. She groaned pitifully when someone brought her morning tea, and flinched visibly after Ujeni later bustled into the room and flung the curtains wide open, letting in the heartless sunlight.

"Come on, girl, you have a press conference in two hours time!" Ujeni informed her. "And what happened to you last night? It was very ill-mannered to leave Chief Atalifu's party without as much as a word of farewell. Maxi and I were forced to make excuses for your rude behaviour when we went to collect you and found you gone. Oh, yes, we understand that you must have been very excited and very tired, but you should have remembered that the Chief is a very influential man who should be treated with respect. Anyway, go and take your bath; and be quick. Maxi will be here soon to do your make-up!"

Adela almost crawled into the bathroom. She had never in her life felt so awful. Apart from a throbbing headache and upset stomach, her limbs were stiff and heavy, and a cloudy, vague memory connected with Byron Warlock teased her mind. But Adela was in no condition to dwell on it. An icy cold shower taken after a hot bath did little to relieve her suffering.

Maxi took one look at her and immediately prescribed a brand of fizzy mineral salts which at least rendered the headache bearable and settled Adela's stomach.

"What it is to be a celebrity!" Maxi gurgled, gently patting Adela's face with a swab of skin-toner. "Look at these fantastic flowers from some of your admirers!"

"They came while she was in the bath, and she hasn't even glanced at them," Ujeni said to Maxi. "I've never known such an ungrateful girl."

Joe and Yoweri tapped on the door while Ujeni was reading the cards attached to the immense bouquets and floral arrangements.

"Just to let you ladies know that the chairman insists that we fly to London with him in his private jet this evening," Joe announced. "He is keen to feature Adela in a television commercial as part of Pan Africa Oil's promotional campaign, and the cameraman he and his board of directors want has only three more days in Britain before flying to Toronto."

"Oh, but Sam is expecting me home!" Ujeni objected. "His niece is getting married."

"You'll have to give it a miss, that's all," Joe said dismissively. "Have Adela ready within the next thirty minutes. It's bad public relations to keep the Press waiting."

"I wanted to go with the other girls to that tented camp in a game park," Adela complained.

"Well, you can't," Maxi retorted before Joe could reply. "Believe me, you'll find London much more exciting," she continued, as Joe nodded.

"Of course you will!" He beamed a self-satisfied smile upon the array of flowers. "And you can expect this sort of VIP treatment all the way."

Then bending to examine a particularly elaborate arrangement of orchids, he said, "These must have cost somebody a packet! I wonder who sent them." Idly, he detached the miniature envelope containing a card. "Byron Warlock," he read. "'Congratulations and best wishes for the future.' Well, well . . . Our girl certainly made an impression in all the right quarters!"

At the mention of Byron's name, Yoweri saw bewilderment cross Adela's face, swiftly followed by an expression of someone trying hard to recapture details of a dream. It was plain to him that the girl was not at all clear of what might have taken place during the previous night, and he congratulated himself on his decision to let sleeping dogs lie.

The press conference proved yet another triumph for Adela. Maxi had cleverly understated her make-up, yet concealed any signs of over-indulgence and fatigue, and made her wear a national costume of pure cream cotton with a narrow border in her country's national colours. The result was one of refreshingly natural beauty.

Another of Maxi's calming pills ensured Adela's relaxed handling of the questions put to her. She was well-schooled in sticking to, as well as elaborating on, the biographic details invented by Joe, and was at one stage of the press conference able to make a little joke about herself which caused the reporters, photographers and television crews to love her.

An Unspoilt Beauty Queen one headline ran, next day, although Adela was not around to read it; and *Adela, Queen of Hearts* screamed another, while her first appearance on the two channels of Kenya television was the highlight of that evening showings.

The rest of Adela's day passed in a flurry of packing, telephoning her mother, Keti and Sam, because everybody was supposed to be at the airport three hours before the Chairman's private jet was due to take off.

The private jet itself was a wonder to behold. Adela had never imagined that a plane could be transformed into a comfortable flying home, and she unashamedly squealed with pleasure as Chief Atalifu proudly led her and her entourage — comprising Ujeni, Joe, Maxi and Yoweri, on a conducted tour. Besides the usual offices, the jet boasted two bedrooms with adjoining bathroom facilities, a fitted kitchen, small dining area and a video-viewing lounge.

"Look at all these videos!" Adela exclaimed, diving forward to inspect the row upon row of cassettes.

"Shall we be able to watch some during the flight?"

"Of course!" the chief laughed. "Take your pick."

Joe held up a warning finger. "Just a minute, Adela. I think Ujeni had better choose for you." He turned to Chief Atalifu and respectfully explained that Adela's video-viewing was restricted as well as censored. "We try our best to prevent her watching videos containing violent or sexually explicit scenes," he said. "We may be old-fashioned in our thinking, but it seems to us that we will never recover the age of innocence if young people are exposed to the filth that passes for entertainment these days."

"But surely she is old enough to think for herself," the chief remarked, reflectively adding, "I've always been of the opinion that over-protectiveness can be just as dangerous, perhaps even more so, than exposure to the realities of the modern world. However . . . " he smiled broadly upon Ujeni, ". . . if the result of your care and protection is this delightfully unspoilt creature whom we're fortunate to have as Miss Pan Africa Oil, then nobody can possibly find fault with your methods."

The company relaxed, and Ujeni, confident of Chief Atalifu's approval, walked over to the rows of cassettes and began reading the titles. "This 'Search for the Golden Ark' looks interesting," she commented. "It's described as an exciting adventure. And see Adela, 'Freedom Fighter' with Byron Warlock. We have watched nearly all his films, but I don't recall this one."

She glanced mischievously at the chief. "I didn't get a chance last night to congratulate Mr. Warlock on the good moral standards of his pictures. I have never seen him in any movie that I'd be ashamed to watch with my own mother!"

"His private life is equally commendable," Chief Atalifu said. "I have known Byron for some years, and I've never ceased to admire him. Which is why I was delighted when he agreed to be a judge in our beauty contest. It's tragic that fate has dealt him such a rough deal."

Yoweli, whose eyes had turned to Adela at the mention of Byron Warlock's name, saw how the girl suddenly stiffened and her face clouded. From the anxious wringing of her hands, he sensed that she burned to know what tragedy affected her hero. So Yoweri, wanting to put an end to her misery and disregarding Joe Banda's earlier instruction that he should not speak unless spoken to, asked the chief what had happened to the movie star.

Chief Atalifu sadly shook his head, and appeared to hesitate before saying "I may as well tell you, since I understand that Byron's agent is on the point of issuing a press statement, and it will be common knowledge in no time."

Remembering his duty as host, he invited everybody to take a seat and called one of his stewards to bring drinks. As soon as they were settled and served, he continued "You surely must have heard about the helicopter crash Byron was involved in some eighteen months ago, while he was filming in Zaire? He was badly injured, and to save his life he was given a blood transfusion at a little up-country hospital prior to being flown down to a South African clinic. Well, to cut a long story short, the blood he was given carried the AIDS virus. Byron is now HIV positive."

Only Yoweri Wamala noticed the effect this information had on Adela. Only he saw from her changing expression that any uncertainty about the previous night's happenings was a thing of the past, that with the sudden clearing of her mind had come a terrifying fear.

Two Years Later

Chapter 12

"I want a divorce," Sam, Ujeni's husband, made the announcement quietly, and his wife of twelve years stared at him in astonishment.

"What on earth for?" she wanted to know.

Sam avoided her startled eyes by getting out of his chair and going to stand with his back towards her at the window.

They were alone in the sitting-room of the vast suite being shared by Joe Banda, Yoweri Wamala, Maxi, Ujeni and Adela at the famous Claridges Hotel in London. All of them were in Britain for the launch of a new range of cosmetics and scent designed especially for the modern black woman by a famous fashion house, and for which Adela was being paid the breathtaking sum of five million dollars to promote over the ensuing two years. On the strength of this windfall, Ujeni had paid for both Sam and Adela's friend Keti to join the group already in London. She had expected Sam to be overcome with gratitude for her generosity. Instead, here he was talking of divorce.

"Go on, tell me," she urged him. "I have always thought that you and I had a good marriage."

"What sort of marriage is it when one partner travels the world, only dropping in on the marital home for a few days every six months or so?" Sam asked. "What sort of marriage is it when all my wife can talk about is the famous people she has met during her travels, and the famous places she has visited? I have repeatedly told you over the phone and by letter that your mother is very sick. She pleads to be allowed to see you and Adela before she dies. Your brother and sisters, like me, find it insulting and shameful that not once since you attached yourself to Joe Banda and his ambitious schemes has Adela been allowed to visit the rest of her family. The clan elders have directed me to bring the girl home for the comfort of her mother."

Ujeni opened her mouth to protest, but Sam silenced her with a sneer. "Don't worry. I know the score. The days are gone when the

95

"About this divorce you're so keen on. There's somebody else, isn't there?..."

elders had authority over folk like you. I'm simply relaying their wishes, for what it's worth."

She glared at his stolid back and said in a harsh voice, "About this divorce you're so keen on. There's somebody else, isn't there? You're putting all the blame on me so that you can sneak off and pretend it's my fault that you have taken another wife."

Sam spun around to face her. "Yes, there is somebody else — but there might not have been if you had behaved as a responsible wife, instead of globe-trotting with the likes of Joe Banda! Look at yourself, Ujeni! Just look at yourself! I scarcely recognise you with your mass of false hair and heavy make-up — and that outfit you're wearing! You'd be a laughing stock back home if you walked around in that!"

Ujeni glared defiantly at him. "How dare you? You forget that you have profited as much from my what you call my globe-trotting with Joe Banda. Oh, yes! You nobly refused shares in the company, but that didn't stop you, my dear husband, from accepting money from me for your completely modernised clinic which allows you to attract the cream of medical school graduates. And you certainly would not be driving the latest model of Mercedes if I hadn't helped you to buy it!"

Sam surveyed her grimly. "Nor would I be living in domestic chaos with lazy servants. I might as well be a bachelor." He went to the door and paused on the threshold. "I'll stay here for the launch for Adela's sake. The girl was thrilled to be united with her old school friend. However, I warn you. As soon as I reach home, I'm starting divorce proceedings on grounds of desertion."

When he had gone, Ujeni paced restlessly around the room. The past two years had passed in a blaze of triumph for Adela and everybody associated with her. After her success as Miss Pan Africa Oil, money had rolled in from her winnings in other international beauty contests, from advertising contracts, from special appearances at important charity functions, from guest appearances in films, from promotions such as the one they were in London to attend. The Miss

World project was regularly shelved because Adela was already earning plenty of money from other enterprises.

Ujeni weighed her marriage against the sophistication and luxury of her present life and found it wanting. The return to a hardworking doctor's wife held not the slightest appeal. She looked around at the sumptuous splendour of a Claridges' suite and smiled. This was now her accustomed setting. Only a fool would sacrifice it for the sake of a disgruntled husband. Let Sam go ahead with the divorce. Ujeni herself was perfectly satisfied with her present situation.

*   *   *

Unaware of the drama taking place in the sitting-room, Adela and Keti were enjoying a good heart-to-heart chat in the privacy of Adela's bedroom. They had much to talk about, because although they had kept in touch by phone and letter, they had not met for two years.

Adela was keen to hear about all her old classmates, and pressed Keti for even the smallest details of life back home. Keti, on her part, was really interested in her friend's travels and the celebrities she had met. After Adela related how she was regularly feted by their country's ambassadors during her visits to various parts of the world, Keti remarked, "So you must have made a wonderful new circle of friends. You've changed, you know. If you came home now, you would probably find us all very dull."

Adela gave a tired shrug. "I doubt it." Then she blurted out, shocking Keti with the bitterness of her tone, "I'm quite sick of always being in the company of Joe, Ujeni and Maxi! You'll never believe it, but Yoweri Wamala, the man who persuaded you and me to enter his silly beauty contest, has turned out to be the only friend I have. How can I make friends if the other three are forever hovering around me like gaolers?"

"But surely you meet lots of girls of your own age at these beauty contests?" Keti tentatively ventured.

"No way!" Adela scoffed. "Maxi sticks to me like a leech! She arranges things so that I can never really talk to other contestants. She and Ujeni choose my clothes, the books I'm allowed to read, and the films and videos I'm allowed to see. Wherever we go, and whoever we meet, they do all the talking." She laughed, but without humour. "I wish you could have been around when I was invited to the film premiere of 'Forbidden Fruits' in Los Angeles! The three of them were torn between our being seen rubbing shoulders with a whole load of celebrities, and not wanting me to watch such a sexy movie. They argued for days. In the end, we attended the premiere. Their instinct for social status overcame any concern that the movie might give me impure ideas!"

Keti was disturbed by Adela's obvious unhappiness. As a great believer in looking on the bright side, she said, "At least you have the consolation of knowing that this can't go on forever. I mean, nobody can expect to be a beauty queen for the rest of her life. And at the end of your career, when you can please yourself by doing what you want to do, I should imagine that you'll be a very rich woman. Then one day a nice, handsome man will come along, marry you, and you'll settle down happily to raise a family."

"I . . . I don't plan on that — the happy marriage bit, I mean," Adela said, before tears filled her eyes and trickled down her cheeks. "There has only ever been one man I . . . I liked . . . To the rest, and I can tell by the way they look at me, all I am is a sort of fancy doll!"

Keti held her tightly as the tears drew forth sobs, and as soon as the sobs died down, said, "We've got to get you out of this. I'll speak to Sam. You can't go on living this useless, artificial life."

Adela merely sighed in acknowledgement and made no resistance as Keti helped her to the bed.

"You rest. I'm going to find Sam and put a stop to this nonsense," Keti told her.

"No need to bother Sam," Adela murmured. "I'll be all right. It's just that these days I'm always so tired. But I feel better after getting that lot off my chest! Keti, you can't imagine how happy I am to have you here . . ." her voice trailed off as she sank into deep sleep.

Keti went in search of Sam. She found him in the hotel foyer, in conversation with what she correctly assumed, from their casual clothes to be African university students. He caught sight of her and beckoned her to join them.

"This is Keti," he introduced her to the three young men and went on to say, "Keti is a very special person. She's a novice in a comparatively new order of nuns who are devoting themselves to the care of AIDS victims. She put in some time at one of their hospices during her school holidays, and now she's at their nurses' training centre. She expects to be working with AIDS orphans before too long."

The young men greeted Keti with respect and made enthusiastic promises of assistance to the nuns as soon as they completed their post-graduate medical studies and went home. Keti was grateful for their promised support, and gladly answered their questions regarding the work of her order, but she urgently needed to talk to Sam about Adela. She breathed a sigh of relief when the young men at last went away, and she allowed Sam to lead her to Claridges' world famous *'art decor'* cocktail lounge.

Sipping an unwanted orange juice, she voiced her fears that Adela was heading for a nervous breakdown. "From what she tells me," Keti said, "these people — and that includes your wife, Adela's sister — treat her like their private property. Did you realise that she's not allowed to make any friends, or that she can't even go shopping on her own?"

Sam toyed with his whisky and soda. "Keti, I advised against it from the start. Ujeni is considerably older than Adela, whom I have known since she was a child. She has been slow to mature, and her development as an adult is being totally distorted by those three money-grabbers. I don't count Yoweri Wamala because from what I've seen of him, he regrets attaching himself to this appalling bandwagon."

100

Keti's face registered exasperation. "Surely you can do something, Sam? Adela is my friend, and I won't rest until she is out of this rat race. She virtually collapsed on me this afternoon. I'm frightened for her."

Sam thought hard for a few minutes, then said, "Go back to Adela's room, and if she is alone and still resting, call me — as an emergency. In your presence, I'll do a thorough examination and take a blood sample. From the look of things, I'd say that she is seriously anaemic. If I'm proved right, I'll insist upon her having at least three months' rest at home. Once we get her home, I'll have my lawyer see what he can do about getting her out of Joe Banda's clutches."

Keti's heart lightened and she sprang from her chair and, to the amazement of those sitting nearby, enveloped Sam in an affectionate hug. "Oh, Sam!" she breathed, "if I wasn't taking Holy Orders, you're exactly the type of man I would want to marry!"

She hurried to Adela and found her still asleep on the bed, in a tense, curled-up position, breathing hoarsely and soaked in sweat. Keti's first thought was pneumonia. She had seen several cases during her short time at the hospice. But it was impossible for her to understand how such an illness could develop in so short a time. Quickly, she picked up the phone, dialled the cocktail lounge and asked to speak to Sam. As soon as he answered her call, she said "Sam, please come at once. This really is an emergency!"

Chapter 13

Sam's verdict after he had examined Adela and taken a blood sample was that her symptoms were those of nervous exhaustion and anaemia rather than pneumonia, although he diagnosed some slight congestion of the lungs. He told Joe Banda so when he met him in the hotel reception where he, Sam, had gone to arrange for the blood sample to be delivered to a laboratory for testing.

"Ordinarily I might have made a guess at malaria, but I know for a fact that she has no history of malarial attacks," Sam said, "and the injection I gave her has reduced her temperature. It seems highly probable that all Adela needs is a good long rest. I'm confining her to bed for the next few days."

Joe stared at him as though Sam had gone mad. "Bed for the next few days? That's impossible!" he exclaimed. "Five million dollars hangs on Adela appearing at the launching this week. Surely you can fix her up so that she can at least . . ."

"Are you crazy?" Sam shouted, regardless of startling other arriving and departing guests. "Didn't you listen to what I have just told you? The girl is ill! She is a nervous wreck, and even before confirmation from the lab, I can tell you that her blood count is dangerously low!"

Joe Banda blustered and argued in vain for a few minutes, then fiercely muttering about interfering medics, he stormed off in search of Maxi.

Drawing the woman into the privacy of his ensuite bathroom, to avoid interruptions or eavesdropping by Ujeni or Yoweri, he said to her, "I've turned a blind eye to what you've been giving Adela before any important appearance, because I'm absolutely against drugs of any kind. However, your future and mine are at stake. Sam insists that Adela stays in bed, claiming that her condition warrants it. He refuses point blank to allow her to attend the launch. Apparently she went down with a fever a couple of hours ago . . ."

"What!" Maxi's eyes widened. "But she was perfectly all right at lunchtime!"

"I know," Joe agreed. "And if you ask me, the girl is putting on an act for the benefit of that friend of hers, and because she enjoys having her brother-in-law fuss over her.

"Well, madam, let's get to the point. A cool five million dollars isn't to be sniffed at, and we can't afford to kiss it goodbye. Once we get our hands on that, we won't need Adela or anybody else. So I'm counting on you to do the necessary and have Adela at the launch of those cosmetics, no matter what you have to do to get her there!"

Maxi regarded Joe with a mixture of amusement and calculation. She of all people knew him for what he was — a complete opportunist, and an exceptionally efficient one at that. Only, for the first time since she had known him, she was the one in a position to call the tune. Maxi enjoyed the feeling of power. "Fifty-fifty?" she mildly enquired of him.

With difficulty, Joe controlled his fury at the advantage she was taking. Grudgingly, he nodded. "Okay. Fifty-fifty."

Maxi smiled sweetly. "Let me have it in writing, Joe, and the deed will be done." She left him cursing silently to himself.

After leaving Joe, and throughout the following two days, Maxi proved herself a competent and conscientious nurse. Sam was openly amazed that such an elegant, worldly woman could so easily turn her hand to the duties of a sick-room. She won his admiration as well as his full confidence when, on her first evening of sharing the nursing with Keti, one of the long fingernails of which she was so proud caught in the loose thread of a blanket while she was making the invalid comfortable and was ripped off well below the quick, yet she insisted upon carrying on.

"You must let me put a plaster on it," Sam had suggested, examining with concern the mutilated finger from which a bead of blood and puss oozed.

"Not on your life!" Maxi had cheerfully replied. "If you wrap it in Elastoplast, how will I be able to disguise the damage with a false fingernail? Don't worry. This sort of thing has happened before, and it's never serious."

She remained cheerful as she attended with Keti to all of Adela's intimate and personal requirements, and Adela came to depend on her more and more for all the small attentions that ease the lot of the bedridden.

In marked contrast to Ujeni, Maxi seldom left Adela for any length of time, leading Sam to remark to Keti, "How badly I misjudged that woman! She is selfless in her devotion to Adela. She's in that room day and night — while Ujeni is too busy shopping for clothes and jewellery to do more than pop her head around the door and ask when Adela will be out of bed!"

Sam was not to know that, besides shopping for clothes and jewellery, Ujeni was also busy putting a great deal of energy into netting Joe Banda whom she had marked out as her next husband. From the beginning of their business relationship, Joe had held a strong attraction for her which she had done her best to hide until now, when her husband threatened — or should it be promised? — to set her free. She was aware that Joe, too, had home commitments in the form of a wife and several children. However, these people tactfully stayed in the background, or were kept there, and Ujeni saw them as no hindrance to her designs on Joe.

Her tactics to win him consisted of never appearing in his company unless she was, by her own standards, impeccably dressed, manicured and coiffured, making his personal comfort a top priority in a manner utterly foreign to the way she had ever treated Sam, and openly siding with him in his opinion that too much fuss was being made of the slight chill from which Adela was apparently suffering.

Ujeni blessed Maxi for keeping busy in the sick-room, leaving her a clear field in which to ensnare Joe, and she was determined to make the most of the heaven-sent opportunity.

Early in the afternoon of the day appointed for the launching of the new range of cosmetics, Maxi, in splendid humour, bossily ordered Sam and Keti to take themselves off on a tour of the city. "You have been in London for almost a week, and have seen nothing!" she pointed out. "What a waste of a visit to this historic city!" She produced six tickets from her purse and spread them out on a coffee table. "Here! These two are for the bus tour of ancient monuments. These two are for a boat trip down the river Thames, stopping off at Hampton Court. And these two are for an evening with King Henry the Eighth and his court at a place called St. Catherine's Dock, where — it says here — you'll eat the roast beef of old England and be entertained by a company of strolling players. How does that strike you?"

Sam smiled at her but shook his head. "How can we leave you to cope alone for all the time this sightseeing will take? It wouldn't be fair. Besides, I'm expecting the results of Adela's blood test sometime today."

Maxi glanced at Adela's sleeping form. "All these tickets were intended for Adela and me. They expire today, so if you two don't use them, they'll be wasted. Both of you need a break, so do me a favour and have a good time — for once! I've already promised Adela that together we shall see the sights and take the boat trip the moment she is well. As for the rest, you know that she's safe with me. If anything goes wrong, I can always call the hotel doctor."

"Maxi!" impulsively, Keti embraced her. "At first I thought that Adela was lonely and unhappy. I worried about her. Now I'm sure that as long as she has you, she will always be safe."

Sam gruffly added, "I second that. And because I agree that it's time for Keti to see more of London than this hotel, we'll take up your very kind offer, Maxi. Thank you."

"Get along and enjoy yourselves," Maxi told them. "The tour bus leaves in about fifteen minutes. The doorman here will tell you where to board it."

On their way to ground level in the lift, Sam said, "It amazes me how a wonderful woman like Maxi got involved with Joe Banda. But I'm glad that she did — for Adela's sake!"

Keti smiled warmly. "It's a relief to know that Adela has such a good friend. Yes, Maxi is remarkable. She was very strict with us when we attended her charm school. I never really liked her, but now I see that it's wrong to judge someone by appearance. Maxi is a very special person."

She would have spoken differently, had she known that no sooner had she and Sam turned their backs than out came Maxi's bag of tricks — a selection of syringes, phials and pills.

First, Maxi gave Adela an injection which revived the girl sufficiently for her to take a bath.

"I feel great!" Adela babbled, climbing out of the tub and jumping up and down in a state of hyper-activity.

"You'll feel even better after swallowing these," Maxi said with a smile as she gave Adela two small white pills. Whatever they were, the pills succeeded in reducing Adela to a more manageable commodity. She gradually settled down so that Maxi was able to work at transforming her gaunt face into a vision of almost ethereal beauty, and hide her neglected hair under a high, flattering turban.

Maxi worked slowly and meticulously, aiming for perfection. By the time she had completed Adela's manicure and pedicure, slipped her feet into jewelled sandals, and draped her in the dramatically voluminous robe of natural raw silk, Maxi had every reason to be satisfied with the results.

"You look absolutely fabulous — a true queen!" she exclaimed, suddenly overwhelmed by what she personally had created from what had once been an ungainly school girl.

They took a taxi to the London Hilton, because Sam had cancelled the Rolls Royce scheduled to collect Adela from Claridges, and arrived to a battery of television and press cameras.

106

"We heard from the doorman that you were ill, Adela!" a reporter familiarly called out. "How are you feeling?"

"Fine! All the better for seeing you!" Adela made the shy, flirtatious rejoinder with a flashing smile.

"That's our girl! another reporter laughed, giving the thumbs-up sign.

She was popular with the Press because she always had an air of being flattered and surprised by their attention.

When they followed her inside, she continued to charm them by posing easily and patiently for dozens of pictures taken to include a display of the range of cosmetics she was promoting.

Afterwards, at the champagne buffet, Adela moved among the invited guests with Maxi close at her side, and behaved with what most people present admiringly saw as her special brand of modest dignity. But the combination of the drugs Maxi administered with the medication prescribed by Sam, was steadily producing a strange and rather frightening effect. She began seeing people as though through the wrong end of a telescope, and while she smiled at remarks made to her she could make no sense of anything said. As the evening wore on, she had to fight off a growing weakness in her limbs, and the effort made her perspire.

Maxi, on the alert for any such distressing signs in her charge, speedily made their farewells to the sponsors and hurriedly escorted Adela out of the hotel and into the nearest taxi.

Joe and Ujeni, who were also at the launch, although careful to keep a discreet distance between Adela and Maxi and themselves, watched their departure and then turned to each other in consternation.

"Supposing she is seriously ill," Ujeni remarked.

Joe chuckled drily, hiding his own anxiety, and patted his pocket. "Everything's here, signed and sealed. We can afford the very best of treatment, if necessary, to get her back to normal. But it's my opinion that Adela's suffering only from a bad attack of influenza. The British climate is notorious for it! She will be perfectly all right in no time. You'll see!"

On their way out of the reception, they almost bumped into Chief Atalifu who greeted them like old friends. "I managed to have a few words with our girl," he confided, "I like to think that Pan Africa Oil played no small part in putting her where she is today! And I'm glad to see that success has not gone to her head — Adela is still the same sweet unspoilt girl. But isn't it time she started putting on a little weight? The ideal African woman should be well-rounded, not like these Westerners who worship lean meat!"

They chatted for a while, then the chief left them to rejoin his hosts with whom he was apparently negotiating a franchise of their products in his own country.

Joe guided Ujeni out to where a car waited to take them back to Claridges.

"It's true what the chief says about Adela," she remarked. "Adela is thinner than she ought to be. I noticed it the other day, when she was having a fitting for a new dress. Maybe she should eat more."

Seated in the car, Joe put his arm around her and gave her a comforting squeeze. "You know as well as I do that Maxi is almost fanatical on the subject of diet. She makes sure that Adela has plenty of protein along with fresh fruit and vegetables. Healthy eating means a healthy mind and body, according to Maxi."

Ujeni smiled at him, and for once there was a trace of malice in the smile. "Then, Joe, I suggest that you adopt the same regime. You really are expanding rather alarmingly around the middle!"

Joe grunted irritably and fell silent for the rest of the journey.

At Claridges reception desk, a curt note was handed to Joe, demanding his and Ujeni's presence in Sam's room as soon as they returned. The pair of them looked at each other and tried to put on brave faces in readiness for the confrontation they anticipated.

"Well, he was sure to find out sometime that Adela had attended the launching. Reports of it will be in all the papers tomorrow," Joe blustered. "And how can he fault us for proving that nothing much is wrong with her?"

Ujeni nervously twisted her fingers. "Except that she wasn't looking too good when Maxi took her out of the reception . . . Supposing she's had some sort of relapse?"

"It got too hot in that place, that's all," Joe argued. "Adela simply wanted a breath of fresh air." He squared his shoulders. "Anyway, I'm not taking any nonsense from that husband of yours. In future, he had better watch his tongue when he is talking to me!"

He marched purposefully towards the lift, and Ujeni followed miserably in his wake.

"I know exactly what you're going to say," he began, intending to gain the upper-hand as soon as they were in Sam's room.

"I very much doubt that you do," Sam said, and Ujeni shrank from the absolute loathing in his tone and expression as his eyes ranged over her and Joe. "If you did, perhaps you wouldn't have gone to such lengths to get me and Keti out of the way so that Adela could be dragged off, by hook or by crook, to promote those cosmetics."

"What do you mean? Okay we fooled you, but we also proved that there's nothing wrong with the girl. She was as right as rain at the launching — everybody said so!" Joe turned to Ujeni to confirm his assertion.

But she was staring hard at her husband, alarmed to notice that Sam's lips trembled and that he was choking back tears. "What is it?" she whispered going to where he stood with bowed head, and taking his hand.

"It's Adela," he mumbled. "The blood test shows that she is HIV positive — and is very likely in the first stages of full-blown AIDS!"

Chapter 14

"Oh, my God!" Joe Banda's agonised cry was wrung from the heart, while Ujeni let out a harsh, strangled sound, finally managing to gasp, "It can't be true!"

Sam, calmer but dejected, slowly nodded, "It's true, all right. As soon as I received the report, I called the lab. They were full of apologies because they have no authority to test for HIV without a patient's permission. The chief technician said that one of his over-enthusiastic assistants was responsible for the slip-up. If it's any consolation, he is firing her. You can thank your lucky stars that Adela's name was not on the sample I sent. If the Press get hold of the story, her life will be hell!"

Joe eagerly snatched at a glimmer of hope. "There must be a mistake. That particular laboratory can hardly be called reliable if people there don't abide by the rules. Who is to say that the assistant didn't also mix-up Adela's blood sample with somebody else's?"

Sam shrugged impatiently. "There's no point in arguing. The only mistake made had nothing to do with the procedure or testing. The laboratory we are talking about has a world-wide reputation for accuracy. Besides, I should have realised that Adela's current illness coincides with the early symptoms of AIDS. I suppose, with her being my sister-in-law and my knowing her as I do, the thought never entered my head."

"AIDS!" Ujeni shrieked. "AIDS! You can't mean it! I swear on my mother's head that my sister has never been near a man in that sense! Joe is right. There's been a terrible mistake."

"It doesn't have to involve sex," Sam wearily explained. "You ought to know by now that you can pick up the HIV virus from infected blood in a blood transfusion, from hyperdermic equipment that's been used by a HIV carrier or full-blown AIDS victim and even from some body fluids if they are allowed to enter a damaged area of your skin like a graze or a cut." He paused. His thoughts immediately flew to

Maxi's torn fingernail and the way she had insisted upon personally laundering the hotel bedsheets after Adela had menstruated and suffered an uncontrollable attack of diarrhoea. He shivered as he recalled her good-natured comment that it was better to hide such embarrassing events from the hotel staff who, despite their surface politeness, probably found it hard to believe that Africans were house-trained.

"I hope you people realise that for your own peace of mind you should be tested for HIV," was all he said.

"What!" Joe Banda collapsed in a terrified, shaking heap into the nearest chair. "Not me! Leave me out of it!"

"Better call Maxi and Yoweri. I'll take the blood samples and they'll only be identified by numbers instead of names at the laboratory." Sam spoke to his wife as though she were a complete stranger, deliberately ignoring her stunned expression. "Oh — and bring Keti. I'll need her help."

When Ujeni led the three into Sam's room — Yoweri curious, Keti concerned, and Maxi defiant and ready to defend her actions of earlier in the evening — there was instant confusion aroused at the sight of Joe Banda, crumpled and blubbering.

"What have you done to him?" Maxi demanded of Sam, but he was already asking Keti about Adela.

"She's sleeping," Keti told him, frowning, "I think you ought to take a look at a rash that's developing on her arms . . ."

Her dreadful suspicion reached him across the room like a laser beam. The strange rash, the herald or symptom of AIDS in full strength!

Sam was too overcome to soften the blow for Maxi and Yoweri. Bluntly, he said "Adela is HIV positive. In fact it's more than likely that she's in the first stages of AIDS. You've all had contact with her, and if you're wise you'll allow me a sample of your blood for testing."

Yoweri stood as if turned to stone, remembering Byron Warlock's furtive, unhappy exit from Adela's room so long ago, and the sympathetic response of the international Press as soon as it was announced that the poor man was HIV positive; while Maxi, staring with horrified eyes at her own still sore finger from which a large part of the nail had so roughly been torn, seemed on the verge of collapse. "It's not possible," she muttered.

Only Keti remained completely calm. She quietly made the sign of the Cross, her lips moving in a silent prayer as she scrubbed her hands before putting on the thin rubber gloves with which Sam supplied her, and helping him arrange his pre-sterilised blood-sample equipment on a convenient table.

Maxi, Ujeni and Yoweri numbly submitted to the needle. They were too much in shock to even think of resisting; but Joe Banda hysterically refused. He backed into a corner, waving his arms as if warding off blows, and claimed, "There's nothing wrong with me! I never had had more than the slightest physical contact with that girl, so you're not scaring me with your talk of blood tests. I'll sue anybody who accuses me of having AIDS!"

"It's best to be on the safe side," Keti gently told him. "Mr. Banda, think of your wife and children at home."

He turned on her with a snarl. "Leave my family out of it!" he snapped. "I tell you I have nothing to worry about! All I ask is that you get that girl as far away from me as possible — as quickly as possible!"

Sam, packing the samples for delivery to the laboratory, raised his head and quietly announced that Adela's condition required the services of a special clinic. "There's an excellent place in Arizona where they have embarked upon research which has so far produced encouraging results. Their form of treatment is quite out of the ordinary, and since they are prolonging the lives of AIDS patients who were without hope, there is every reason to believe that they may eventually produce a curative vaccine. It also has the advantage of being very private in that no word of their patients' identities — and some of them are world famous — is ever leaked to the Press," he said, adding, "Of course, it's expensive, but I take it that Adela has made enough money from this Beauty Queen business to cover the costs of treatment there!"

Joe Banda dabbed at his sweating face with a large handkerchief and rushed to grab the opportunity of off-loading the productive asset which had suddenly turned into a nightmare of a liability. "Of course, of course," he babbled. "I can promise that there will be money for any treatment she requires. How soon can you get her there? Can she leave tomorrow? You'll have to sneak her away without the Press getting to know about it!"

"Yes, but surely she has money of her own?" Sam glanced questioningly at his wife.

Ujeni played nervously with a fringe on her over-elaborate dress.

"Adela has shares in the company, the company we formed to promote her — like the rest of us, except for Yoweri. He's on a straight salary."

"And what about dividends? Most companies pay dividends to shareholders, and you can't say that this company of yours was ever running at a loss," Sam pressed. "Adela must surely have a bank account for her dividends?"

"It doesn't work quite like that," Ujeni murmured.

Joe immediately put in. "No, it doesn't. Our overall expenses are extremely high. But don't you worry, Sam, Adela's medical expenses will be covered. Just get her out of here as soon as you can."

Late as it was, Sam, wishing to avoid gossip among the hotel staff, personally delivered the blood samples to the laboratory, thankful that it stayed open all night. Then, he collected a vast selection of expensive drugs on his own prescription from an all-night chemist, and went for a drink in a cosy little bar not far from Claridges hotel. He needed to sort out his anger and his thoughts. 'How, for instance, was he to break the appalling news to Adela herself and to her parents?' No matter how accidentally the catastrophe had occurred, he placed the blame firmly on Joe Banda, for who else was responsible for taking a raw, impressionable schoolgirl and turning her into a well-travelled celebrity open to God knows what dangers? Had Adela remained at home, none of this would have happened, Sam bitterly told himself. He was additionally uneasy on Adela's behalf about the chances of her gaining access to the vast amounts of money she had undoubtedly earned. Despite Joe Banda's bland assurances, Sam simply did not trust the man.

Sam sipped his drink and tried to concentrate on the arrangements to be made for Adela's admission to the Arizona clinic where AIDS patients could be sure of receiving the best and most up-to-date treatment available. It was at this point that he remembered Keti's suggestion that he should examine the rash on Adela's arms, so he finished his drink and almost ran to the hotel. Although the rash could be an ominous symptom, Sam hoped to subdue it with a new drug included amongst those he had acquired from the all-night chemist.

The moment he opened Adela's room, her wild, abandoned, grief engulfed him. Keti was there, trying to restrain her, as she thrashed around the bed, from tearing out her hair and making bloody furrows down her cheeks which she clawed with her fingernails.

"Stay clear of that blood!" Sam shouted at the sight of Keti trying to immobilise Adela's hands in a bedsheet.

"You see — it's true!" Adela shrieked, "I've got AIDS, haven't I? I'm dying, aren't I?"

She subsided in a sobbing heap, and Sam whispered to Keti "What happened?" Silently, Keti indicated a newspaper scattered on the rug beside the bed. He picked it up and turned to the front page. There, as headlines, was the announcement of Byron Warlock's death from AIDS.

"What has this got to do with it?" Sam asked puzzled, as he stared down at the distraught figure of his sister-in-law.

114

Adela abruptly stopped crying and sat up in bed. Tremors continued to wrack her fragile frame, and she stared blindly at the wall opposite. "It has everything to do with it," she whispered. "And it's my own fault. I might as well tell you, if only to keep you both from thinking I have been sleeping around. Byron was the first and the last."

"But how . . ." Sam began.

Adela impatiently shook her head. "It just happened, that's all," she said. "He was a judge at my very first beauty contest — remember the Pan Africa Oil event in Nairobi? Even now, I'm not too clear about how I came to have the great Byron Warlock all to myself, but I do know that he was every bit as wonderful as all of us at St. Mary's High school ever dreamed him to be. Really beautiful in every way. Most wonderful of all was that it happened on one of the very few times I was able to do exactly as I pleased, and I was there alone with Byron Warlock, the beautiful man I had watched so often on the screen. It was like a dream. I thought next day that it had been a dream. The upsetting part was remembering how Byron cried. I knew that it wasn't a dream as soon as Chief Atalifu told us that because of some blood Byron was given after an accident he was HIV positive. As soon as the chief spoke, it was like a curtain lifting on my memory, and I was terrified."

Sam groaned, and Adela smiled strangely at him. "You know, in a short while I stopped being frightened because I was still the same, and I honestly believed that I couldn't have caught anything from him. After all, we only did it once! But I was wrong, wasn't I, Sam? I've got AIDS, haven't I?"

Tears poured down Keti's face, and Sam could only hang his head miserably.

Adela went to pat his hand, then drew back her own, saying, "I must remember not to touch other people if I don't want to pass this thing on . . . you needn't say anything. If I hadn't guessed what was wrong with me as soon as I read about poor Byron — all this feeling weak, and having to make a dash for the nearest lavatory — I would have known just now when you shouted at Keti to keep away from this blood on my hands."

She held her hands in front of her face and inspected the traces of blood embedded in her fingernails. "You couldn't tell from looking at it, could you? It looks just like everybody else's. Yet the thing that killed Byron, and is all set to kill me is right there, isn't it? That HIV virus — it's there in my blood, alive and well, isn't it? And it is killing me, isn't it?"

Adela's voice rose in anguish and ended in a hopeless sob. Keti said helplessly, "Please, Adela, don't upset yourself."

Sam cleared his throat and said, "Now that you know the score, Adela, I'm arranging for you to have treatment in one of the world's most advanced clinics in the treatment of AIDS. I can guarantee that they will enable you to live as normal a life as possible, and probably extend your life expectancy. So, you see, all is not lost."

Adela looked him straight in the face, unnaturally calm. "All is not lost?" she echoed. "I suppose that all is not lost if you consider living normally as not daring to get too near other people, or marry, or have children. As for my life expectancy, be truthful Sam. Byron must have been able to afford the most expensive treatment in the world, yet he's dead."

"You mustn't give up hope Adela," Keti admonished her. "Sooner or later a cure for AIDS will be found. Researchers are working on it all the time."

Sam methodically made Adela swallow some of the pills he had brought, and prepared to leave. He forced himself to put on an optimistic face as he said, "Keti is right. You must never stop hoping for a cure. Now I have to send off some faxes to the clinic and to the people who run a flying medical service. If all goes well, we should be on our way to Arizona tomorrow."

116

Chapter 15

Adela had been in the Arizona clinic for six months. Sam and Keti had accompanied her there in a flying medical services plane, but could spare only two days of their time in which to see her settled, before returning to Matola by a more conventional airline. Their last sight of her was of a pathetically listless creature lying in bed, the doll Lulu at her side, in a bright, airy room. Dr. Flagstone, the physician in charge, had assured them that Adela would soon be up and about. He had congratulated Sam on already having prescribed drugs that had succeeded in controlling the worst of her symptoms: the general weakness in the limbs, diarrhoea and the frequent high temperature.

The clinic itself had impressed Sam and Keti in different ways; Sam with its state-of-the-art research centre and revolutionary treatment of AIDS and Keti with its serene, optimistic atmosphere, and the loving care with which patients were tended. She also fell in love with the surrounding Arizona desert, recognising that patients could benefit spiritually from its peaceful arid landscape and crisp dry air.

During the first five months, reports on Adela's progress were encouraging. True to Dr. Flagstone's prediction, she was up and about, and her letters spoke of her running informal courses in skin and hair care for some of the other female patients, as well as enjoying desert picnics and riding a bicycle around the clinic's extensive grounds.

Then things started to go sour. Apart from the disturbing news that Adela had developed a chest infection and was confined to bed, almost as alarming, Joe Banda had stopped paying the clinic's bills.

Sam was aware from his wife's infrequent letters that Joe was involved in a legal battle with the fashion house to which Adela was under contract to promote their range of cosmetics.

Apparently Joe, unwilling to refund the two and half million dollars already paid, had first persuaded the sponsors that she was temporarily resting under doctor's orders, but as time went by with no sign of Adela fulfilling her obligations to them, the sponsors had taken legal action to recover their money. Maxi and Yoweri had abandoned Joe and returned home soon after their blood tests and Ujeni's were pronounced HIV negative.

All three of them had been advised to have further tests after six months, and Sam had had the unpleasant task of telling Maxi that in her case a second test was not merely advisable but essential.

With Adela no longer available, Maxi and Yoweri saw little point in staying to watch Joe Banda doing his best to wriggle out of what was obviously turning into a nasty situation. So Maxi was once more holding the reins of her charm school in place of the manager she had appointed to take charge during her absence, and Yoweri was using the money he had earned in Joe's employ to organise more streamlined versions of his former beauty contests all over the country.

Sam decided, although he no longer trusted the woman, to consult Maxi regarding Adela's personal finances, since he was convinced that his sister-in-law must have saved something from her vast earnings. When approached on the subject by letter, Adela had revealed astonishing ignorance of both her earnings and savings. True, she seemed to think that she had some money somewhere because Joe Banda and Ujeni had often talked about setting up a trust fund for her, but other than that, she had no more information.

Sam was sure that Maxi would know all about it, so he effectively hid his distaste as he entered her office, and greeted her with formal courtesy. But his natural good manners faltered as he learned from her that his sister-in-law was, to all intents and purposes, penniless.

Maxi revealed how Joe Banda had craftily worked on the company's accounts to show a consistent loss, hiding the profits in a mass of fictitious expenses. "The expenses for practically everything Adela was involved in were fully paid for by sponsors," she revealed. "And Joe made various investments with most of the money she earned to reap substantial profits."

"Well, surely Adela can claim part of those profits?" Sam argued.

Maxi raised her eyebrows in mock amazement. "You weren't listening, were you? Adela and the company are one. On paper, the company is broke, so Adela is also broke. As for Joe's investments, he has covered his tracks with extreme care. It would take a miracle to trace them."

"But you and my wife, Ujeni?" Sam persisted. "I can't see the pair of you sitting back and quietly watching this . . . this deception taking place. You must have got something out of it surely," Sam pressed on.

Maxi's face hardened. "I have known Joe for a very long time, and I know how he operates. I made it my business to ensure that I got my share of the pickings. After all, I made that girl. Without me, she would never have made it to the top. I earned every cent I got out of turning her into a beauty queen," she said laughing coarsely. "As for your wife! You have only to look at your smart car and clinic to realise that she didn't lose anything on the deal. She was supposed to be employed as Adela's official chaperon, but the only chaperoning she ever did was to chaperon Joe!"

Sam realised that he was getting nowhere, and turned to leave. Maxi detained him as he reached the door. "One more thing," she said, "I took your advice and had another test last week. I'm HIV positive!"

Sam spun around and opened his mouth to express his inadequate sympathy, but Maxi forestalled him. "Save your pity," she snarled. "Save it for the good, decent man who has shared my bed for the past five months, and who is probably infected as well. Please understand that whatever money I made from your sister-in-law's beauty career could never be enough to compensate me for my life and his. I am paying for her success in the hardest possible way, so who can blame me for using that money for the trip of a lifetime? He and I are going around the world — first class all the way — before AIDS has time to turn us both into helpless cripples!"

Sam left her office in a blind rage against fate and the ambitions of Joe Banda. At his house he immediately telephoned the young woman he hoped to marry as soon as his divorce from Ujeni came through, postponing their evening appointment. Then he called the AIDS hospice where Keti was working as a novice-nun, and asked to speak to her.

Keti, after listening to Sam's bitter story of Joe Banda's underhand dealings and gross deception, and Maxi's sad plight, said "Adela will have to come home. There's nothing else for it, Sam. The clinic won't keep her in Arizona indefinitely if the bills aren't being paid. All we can do for Maxi and her friend is pray that the HIV stays dormant."

"Yes, but have you any idea how much it's going to cost to settle the clinic's bills and bring Adela home?" he cried desperately. "I doubt that any normal airline will willingly carry a passenger who is obviously suffering from AIDS — you surely know how the Americans are about that sort of thing! And the flying medical service is quite beyond my means!"

"What about Adela's parents and the rest of her family?" Keti suggested. "They will have to know sooner or later about her condition. We can't go on forever pretending that she's holidaying in the United States. I think you ought to give it to them straight. They are good Christian people, and they are certainly not short of money. I think they will be only too anxious to have their daughter back home. Go and talk to them."

The following day Sam visited his in-laws. Regardless of Keti's insistence that they were good Christians, Sam's personal knowledge of his father-in-law made him dread having to explain the reason for Adela's prolonged stay in the United States.

The interview had an ominous beginning. For a start, the father-in-law openly sneered at Sam's gleaming Mercedes Benz. "I'm glad somebody profited from my youngest daughter's so-called career!" he remarked. "Her mother and I are lucky to get a Christmas card!"

"That's not true," the mother protested. "You know very well that Adela is always sending presents."

120

To Sam, she said, "I must show you that beautiful dinner service she sent us from Paris! It's so delicate that we have only dared use it once!"

"Yes, and how long is it since you saw her?" the father jeered. "She doesn't even acknowledge that she belongs to this family. Oh, I have seen a few foreign newspapers, and I'm flattered to learn that I'm a roving diplomat of aristocratic beginnings, instead of a hardworking coffee farmer from good peasant stock! The folks around here think it is one hell of a joke!"

His wife motioned him to be quiet and offered Sam tea. "It's very nice to see you," she said. "Have you heard from Ujeni lately? Her last letter was all about the wonderful time she was having in London. Why isn't she in America with Adela?"

As the tea arrived and was served, Sam said, "I am here to see you about Adela."

"Yes?" the mother hopefully queried, while the father stiffened almost as if he knew what was coming.

"Yes," Sam continued, trying to keep a tremor out of his voice. "I'm afraid I have bad news . . . Adela has AIDS and we have to bring her out of the clinic where she is being treated because the bills aren't being paid!"

The mother's cup slipped from her suddenly trembling hands and shattered at her feet. The father, bewildered, glanced hopelessly around the sitting-room, as though looking for a means of escape.

"No! No! Not my baby!" the mother moaned.

Sam rushed in with, "Look, it will be all right. I promise that I'll make sure she gets the medication she needs . . ."

"She is not coming here!" the father hoarsely stated. "We weren't good enough for her when she was travelling the world as a beauty queen, so she is not coming here for everybody we know to point the finger at us and treat us like lepers! And you needn't go bothering her brother and sisters. Like us, they have been kept well out of her glamorous life. You'll get no help from them!"

Sam stared at him and gulped. This was turning out to be far worse than he had anticipated. "She has nowhere else to go," he said, "and I came here hoping that the family would be prepared to at least pay part of the cost of bringing her back to Matola."

"Not I," the father regarded him stonily. "I'm having nothing to do with it. We were pushed aside when she teamed up with that Joe Banda. Let him take care of her. He is probably responsible for her AIDS! And, as I've just told you, forget about asking her brother and sisters — they are still smarting from the snubs they have received."

Sam could have hit him. He might have done, had not the mother appealed to his pity. The poor woman sat hunched in her chair, the picture of despair, wailing. "God have mercy! God have mercy on my child!"

"Get out, now that we've heard what you had to say," the father told him. "Get out and never return to my house. My youngest daughter is already dead as far as we are concerned, and we never want to see you or your wife again!"

Sam was forced to clench his fists on the steering wheel to prevent them from shaking as he drove to the AIDS hospice to see Keti. She got permission from the Sister-in-Charge to talk to him in a quiet corner of the hospice garden, and immediately they were seated on a wooden bench, he slumped forward, clutching his head in his hands. It was not necessary for him to tell her of the fruitless outcome of his visit to his in-laws. Every line of his body indicated defeat. Keti sympathetically took his hand and said, "Once we get Adela home, there will be a place for her here. I'm sure of it. We are a poor Order, but Mother Superior would never refuse a destitute patient."

Sam snorted angrily. "Destitute! Who would believe that six months ago that same girl lived in the lap of luxury and had the world at her feet?" He asked sighing wearily. "There's only one thing for it, Keti. I'm going to have to sell the Mercedes and mortgage the house to raise

... the father told him ". . my youngest daughter is already dead as far as we are concerned..."

the money for Adela's medical bills and flight home. It's only fair, considering that the car was paid for out of Adela's earnings."

"There must be some other ways," Keti objected. "Can't you contact Ujeni and get her to persuade Joe Banda to pay up? Nobody is completely bad, Sam, and I'm sure that Joe Banda's conscience will eventually lead him to do the right thing."

"I faxed Ujeni and tried to telephone her last week. She and Banda are no longer at the flat they were renting. They have moved out without leaving a forwarding address," he said. "In any event, I have no faith in Banda's conscience. I would be surprised to find he had one. No, Keti. I'll arrange to get rid of the car tomorrow, and see about mortgaging the house. Meanwhile, I hope you can obtain permission to travel to the States with me. I don't think I can face the journey on my own."

Keti sadly watched him drive away, then went into the hospice's tiny chapel to pray for him, her sick friend Adela and for Maxi and her man friend.

During the drive home, Sam was busy calculating mentally the size of mortgage he could expect to raise on his house, and how much the Mercedes Benz might fetch on the second-hand car market. Set against the figures he arrived at were the Arizona clinic's fees which increased with every day that Adela remained there, normal one-way air fafes for himself and Keti, if she was allowed to accompany him, and the cost of hiring a special plane for them to bring Adela back to Matola.

Altogether, Sam feared that the money from a mortgage on the house and the sale of the car might be insufficient to cover the total expenses, and that it might be necessary to raise another mortgage on his clinic. There yet again he had Adela to thank for the clinic's up-to-date facilities.

His future did indeed seem bleak. Sam coldly accepted that for the next five to ten years he would be working primarily to pay off the mortgage or mortgages at a high rate of interest before his property was once more truly his.

His mind was so overwhelmed with money problems that he failed to notice the visitor sitting forlornly on his doorstep until he had parked the car and was mounting the verandah steps. Then he gasped "Ujeni! When did you get here?"

His wife rose shakily to her feet and made as if to embrace him, but Sam swiftly side-stepped her outstretched arms. "Oh, Sam!" she exclaimed, "I've been here for hours, and there was nobody to let me into the house."

"I know," Sam said, unlocking the door. "The servants go off as soon as I turn my back. You had better come in. I hope you'll excuse the mess."

She did not remark upon the obvious neglect of her once perfect home, although her nose wrinkled at the stale dusty smell of the place.

Pouring drinks for both of them, Sam pointedly asked Ujeni what had brought about this unexpected visit, and whether she had by any chance come with the news that Adela's medical expenses were being paid in full.

In response, she stared at her feet and took a long gulp at her drink before saying, "This is no visit. I'm home to stay. I can't tell you anything about the medical expenses. Joe dumped me. The law suit with the fashion house got too complicated even for him to handle, so he simply disappeared, leaving me with a one-way ticket to Matola, and just enough cash to get me to London airport. I put my bags in Left-Luggage when I landed here, and came into town on the bus."

She favoured her husband with an apologetic smile. "I have been a fool, Sam, and I'm sorry. Can you forgive me? Can we start all over again?"

Chapter 16

It was early evening when Sam and Keti arrived at the clinic in Arizona. The trans-atlantic flight coupled with subsequent legs of the journey by long distance bus to the place had left them dispirited and exhausted. Dr. Flagstone, himself looking unusually anxious, not to mention embarrassed, took one look at their tired, worried faces, and immediately insisted that they be given a meal and allotted self-contained rooms.

"It's a relaxing bath and early to bed for you people," he declared. "Tomorrow will be soon enough for you to see Adela and discuss arrangements for her travel."

They gave in without argument. Keti was almost asleep on her feet, while Sam needed time alone to collect his muddled thoughts.

From the moment that Ujeni had stepped back into his life, his troubles had multiplied. Her assumption that the two of them could easily slip back into the way things were before she took up with Joe Banda received a nasty knock when Sam revealed that the house was to be mortgaged, and that although he was no longer in a position to pay for a divorce he did not want her as his wife. Besides, any chance of reconciliation was forever lost, had she but known it, as soon as she expressed indignation that he was ready to forfeit everything he owned to bring her sister home.

"Don't be ridiculous!" she had snapped. "What is the point of going broke to bring Adela to Matola when she is going to die anyway? Let her die in the States. It won't make any difference to her. It's the living you should be thinking about. And, remember, whatever your plans concerning the end of our marriage, you will still have to support me!"

Sam's disgust at Ujeni's selfishness was strengthened by her determination to break up his relationship with the young woman whom he had planned to marry. As well as taking up residence in his house as of right, she lost no time in gaining the support of the Church in the fight to save her marriage. Sam, who had moved into a hotel soon after Ujeni revealed her intention of staying put in the house, was nearly driven mad by priests popping in at all hours of the day and night to remind him of his marriage vows, the Church's non-acceptance of divorce, and to attempt persuading him to return home. In the two weeks prior to his and Keti's departure for Arizona, his work had suffered through lack of sleep, and he often felt that life was not worth living.

Sheer weariness ensured that Sam slept well on that first night at the clinic in the Arizona desert. He awoke to sparkling sunlight and a cool breeze blowing through an open window. For the first time since the reappearance of his wife, his heart lightened. In a sudden mood of optimism, Sam stopped feeling sorry for himself and smilingly started counting his blessings: this was something taught him years ago by his mother whenever he faced childhood disappointments. He mentally listed his blessings as having successfully managed to raise enough money to take Adela home; the AIDS hospice in Matola being willing to accept Adela as a patient; the promise to stand by him through thick and thin made by the young woman whom he hoped one day to marry; and the confidence that if he worked doubly hard he might be able to pay off the mortgages on the house and clinic in record time.

He and Keti met over breakfast and then joined Dr. Flagstone in his office. It was an awkward little get-together, with the doctor having to explain that since his clinic was a registered company with profits meant to finance further research as well as shareholders looking to substantial dividends, it could not be possible to retain a patient free of charge. The man was sad to see Adela go, but what could he do?

"How soon can we see Adela?" Keti wanted to know. "Does she know that we're here?"

Dr. Flagstone replied, "Yes, she knows you have arrived, and she's naturally just as keen to see you." He paused uncomfortably before speaking directly to Sam. "Look, I won't beat about the bush. Adela's progress has been excellent until recently. Her response to a new course of treatment even led us to believe that we were on the verge of a cure for AIDS."

"Then what?" Sam asked quietly, sensing bad news ahead.

The doctor sighed. "Then, as luck would have it, and against all the rules of this establishment, on one of the desert picnics we organise from time to time, she made friends with a family touring in a trailer and who were parked near our picnic site. Nurse Simmons assures me that Adela could not have spent more than ten minutes with these people, but she considered it necessary to report the encounter to me because one of the children belonging to the family had a hacking cough and a runny nose."

Keti gripped the arms of her chair, and gasped, while Sam swallowed hard and said, "You mean Adela has picked up an infection?"

The doctor slowly nodded. "We were encouraged to believe that we had found a way to boost her immunity system. Unfortunately, we have been proved wrong. A week after the picnic she developed a rising temperature and breathing problems.

"What's her condition at the moment?" Sam asked.

"Pretty bad," the doctor admitted. "There are signs of kidney failure. AIDS strikes in very capricious ways."

He accompanied them to the room which Adela had occupied since being admitted to the clinic. During the past six months, she had firmly stamped her personality on it. The dressing-table held a neat array of creams, lotions and cosmetics, a flowering plant stood on the window ledge, along with a framed photograph of her mother, brother and sisters; and Lulu the doll, wearing the Matola national costume, sat sedately in an easy chair.

The disturbing notes were the bleeping monitor, the breathing apparatus, and the drip inserted in Adela's arm as she lay motionless on the bed with an oxygen mask half-obscuring her face.

She opened her eyes as Keti and Sam entered the room, and managed a weak smile. Keti took her hand and said, "We have come to take you home."

Two days later the three of them were aboard the medical services plane that had landed on the clinic's private airstrip. Adela had been carried aboard on a stretcher and was still attached to a drip. Dr. Flagstone had also supplied Sam with the drugs she was likely to need during the flight, and two paramedics, employees of the medical services company, were in attendance.

Keti stayed at Adela's side for most of the fifteen hour journey to Matola, allowing Sam to take her place only during the two refuelling stops. As she watched over her heavily-sedated friend, Keti remembered their carefree schooldays, their incredible plans for the future, and the way their lives had taken such different, extraordinary paths. She recognised little of the schoolgirl Adela in the gaunt, panting figure on the narrow airplane bunk.

Sam had arranged for an ambulance to be waiting for them when they landed in Matola, but he received a rude shock. The ambulance attendants flatly refused to have anything to do with an AIDS patient: and since the disease was so rife in the country, they had no difficulty spotting one. Sam argued, threatened and, in desperation, tried bribing. Nothing he said, however, had the least effect. The ambulance attendants, with the connivance of the driver, aggressively stated their case for protecting themselves, their families, and future patients to be transported in their vehicle, then drove off in self-righteous fury.

So it was that Adela, Keti and Sam arrived at the AIDS hospice on the back of a lorry carrying sacks of charcoal, and for which Sam had paid a ridiculously high bribe.

Mother Superior met them at the door and personally supervised Adela's being bedded down in a ward containing twelve other beds.

Although grateful to this humble sanctuary for taking in his sister-in-law, Sam was secretly appalled at the obvious poverty of the place. There was no running water, and the latrines available to patients capable of walking lay at the far end of the over-grown garden. Bedsheets and blankets were in short supply, so that several patients in the same ward as Adela lay on bare mattresses with odd lengths of what looked to Sam like curtain material to cover themselves. Thanks to the thoughtfulness of Keti's mother, Adela had a full complement of pillows, sheets and blankets.

Mother Superior was acutely aware of his dismay. Her gentle face clouded as she remarked, "It's the best we can do. Most of our patients have been completely abandoned by their families, and you would be surprised at how reluctant the local people are to support our project. The general feeling seems to be that these poor souls brought about their sufferings through their own misbehaviour. Yet most of the women in this ward have been infected with the HIV virus by unfaithful husbands or boyfriends."

"The home for AIDS orphans is well-supported," Sam pointed out.

"Oh, yes," Mother Superior replied. "The babies are regarded, and rightly so, as totally innocent victims."

Sam worried over how his pampered sister-in-law would adjust to the hospice's primitive conditions as he reconnected her drip. Not that Adela appeared conscious of the drastic change in her surroundings. She lay propped up against a pile of pillows, fighting for breath in between calling for a bedpan. The diarrhoea had attacked in full force while they were travelling in the back of the lorry, and Keti had undertaken to clean Adela up before they arrived at the hospice. Now Adela writhed in another attack.

But the worst was still to come. Until Sam could acquire a dialysis machine to replace her steadily malfunctioning kidneys, she was dependent upon the drugs supplied by the Arizona clinic, and these were gradually proving ineffectual. He wasted hours of his precious time in trying to borrow such a machine from the hospitals in and around the capital city. As the various hospital authorities rightly explained, a dialysis machine used to ease the sufferings of an AIDS patient was virtually useless thereafter because complete sterilisation of the equipment could not be guaranteed, making it unsafe for future AIDS-free kidney patients in desperate need of it.

When Sam attempted to buy one from a medical supplies firm, he discovered to his horror that the price was more than the worth of his house. His own clinic was left to his subordinates as he ran from place to place, frantically searching for the only item that might prolong Adela's life.

Everyday, Sam visited the hospice to see Adela, and his fears for her grew as he watched her change into a grotesque caricature of what was once a beauty queen. The skin stretched tight over her fleshless bones, and she was constantly distressed at being incontinent now that she was too weak to walk to the communal latrines. Although the nuns did their best to keep her dry and clean, bedsores soon appeared in the area of her non-existent buttocks. On one frightening occasion, when Sam was present during the dressing of the bedsores, he was physically sick as a small exposed bone of Adela's coccyx, the base of her spine, came away and was, with the aid of forceps, dropped with an inhuman clink into the metal kidney dish holding soiled dressings. Nowadays she was permanently attached to an oxygen cylinder to assist her breathing, and the awareness of her abominable situation was reflected in her frightened and humiliated eyes.

Keti spent as much time as she could with her, spoon-feeding her or simply sitting at the bedside, holding Adela's hand. It saddened her that Adela's brother and sisters, including Ujeni, should pay occasional flying visits to the hospice to leave flowers and fruit, but never to visit the patient. The excuse being that they did not wish to disturb her. But try as she did, Keti could not hide her grief on the evening that she discovered that Adela's eyesight was fast failing.

Sam sought out Mother Superior. "It's time to let her go," he announced.

"Not in my hospice!" Mother Superior indignantly retorted. "Here, we do our best to keep our patients alive. That is the law of God!"

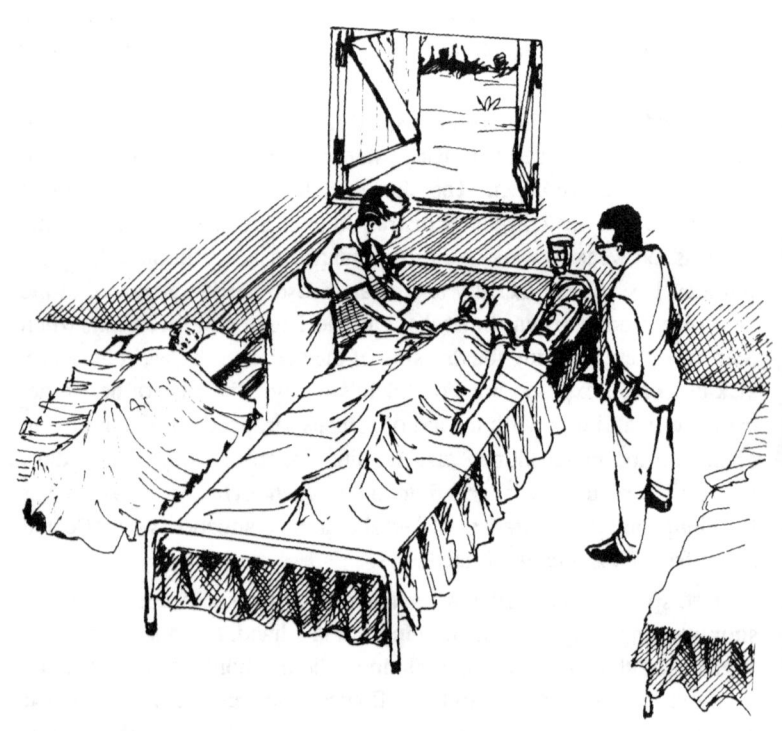

Suddenly Sam was also at the bedside.

"Mother Superior!" Sam pleaded. "I know how you feel, but I'm begging you to let Adela go. I can make her as comfortable as possible, and allow her to float peacefully into oblivion."

"Euthanasia!" Mother Superior spat at him. "Our Church ranks that practice with murder!"

She turned on her heel and left him feeling wretched.

That same night Keti kept another vigil beside Adela's bed. Unrestrained tears flowed down her cheeks as she watched her friend struggle to breath in the oxygen through the mask and tank, while one hand weakly groped the blanket.

Suddenly Sam was also at the bedside. His haggard face revealed his own lack of sleep. "Get some rest, Keti," he said. "I'll call you if there is any change."

Keti struggled through her tears to tell him that Adela urgently wanted something. "I know she does," she gulped, "because her hands are searching for something among the bedding, and her poor sightless eyes are striving to see whatever it is she wants!"

Sam did not hesitate. He went to a roughly-painted chest of drawers and retrieved Lulu, beautifully gowned in elaborate brocade, sitting placidly on top of this piece of furniture, and totally out of place in such an area of poverty-stricken suffering.

"This is what Adela wants." he said, placing the doll in the crook of Adela's arm.

As Sam and Keti watched, a sigh escaped her. She moved the doll until its head nestled beneath her chin, then she feebly edged the oxygen mask away from her face and gave a tired smile.

Neither Keti nor Sam made an effort to restore the life-giving mask. Automatically they reached for each others' hands and watched what had once been a vibrant beauty queen breathe her last few agonising breaths.